Stepping up their game
could have consequences...

THE DATING
DARE

BARBARA DUNLOP
NEW YORK TIMES BESTSELLING AUTHOR

⟨H⟩ HARLEQUIN
DESIRE

Luxury, scandal, desire—welcome to the lives of the American elite.

Be transported to the worlds of oil barons, family dynasties, moguls and celebrities. Get ready for juicy plot twists, delicious sensuality and intriguing scandal.

AVAILABLE THIS MONTH

SECRET HEIR SEDUCTION
REESE RYAN

RECLAIMING HIS LEGACY
DANI WADE

HEARTBREAKER
JOANNE ROCK

ONE NIGHT WITH HIS RIVAL
ROBYN GRADY

JET SET CONFESSIONS
MAUREEN CHILD

THE DATING DARE
BARBARA DUNLOP

ISBN-13: 978-1-335-20900-9
50525
EAN

BARBARA DUNLOP

THE DATING DARE

Recycling programs
for this product may
not exist in your area.

ISBN-13: 978-1-335-20900-9

The Dating Dare

Harlequin Enterprises ULC
22 Adelaide St. West, 40th Floor
Toronto, Ontario M5H 4E3, Canada
www.Harlequin.com

Printed in U.S.A.

"Something's wrong. What's wrong?"

"Nothing. We're shopping," Jamie said. "You're right. We both need a more extensive new wardrobe. I hope you're not planning to bargain hunt."

"I'm not. You've convinced me to spend the investment profits. At least, you've convinced Tasha. Turns out she's not as scrupulous as me."

"You are Tasha."

"You know what I mean."

"What about shirtdresses? I read they're a thing."

"Jamie, stop."

He clamped his jaw, but he stopped.

"Look at me. Is it the kiss? Are you being like this because we kissed each other?"

He didn't answer. And he sure didn't look happy that I'd brought it up.

"It was a kiss. A simple kiss. We've been turning each other into the image we think will attract the opposite sex. All that kiss meant was that it's working. It's working, and that's a good thing."

* * *

The Dating Dare by Barbara Dunlop is part of the Gambling Men series.

Dear Reader,

Welcome to *The Dating Dare*, book two of the Gambling Men series.

When economist James Gillen was left at the altar in book one of the series, I knew he needed his own happy ending. Serendipitously, bridesmaid and librarian Natasha Remington was also recently jilted and available to share empathy.

Together, James and Nat decide they each need an image upgrade to attract the opposite sex. They change their names to Jamie and Tasha, upgrade their appearances, take chances on the stock market and make a ton of money. They also take on new and exciting adventures. Their efforts work—better than either of them ever expected.

I hope you enjoy the story!

Barbara

New York Times and *USA TODAY* bestselling author **Barbara Dunlop** has written more than forty novels for Harlequin, including the acclaimed Chicago Sons series for Harlequin Desire. Her sexy, lighthearted stories regularly hit bestseller lists. Barbara is a three-time finalist for the Romance Writers of America's RITA® Award.

Books by Barbara Dunlop

Harlequin Desire

Chicago Sons

Sex, Lies and the CEO
Seduced by the CEO
A Bargain with the Boss
His Stolen Bride

Gambling Men

The Twin Switch
The Dating Dare

Visit her Author Profile page at Harlequin.com, or barbaradunlop.com, for more titles.

You can also find Barbara Dunlop on Facebook, along with other Harlequin Desire authors, at Facebook.com/harlequindesireauthors!

For all my friends at the office.

One

It wasn't like I was completely alone.

I had friends at work. Well, acquaintances really. But some of us exchanged Christmas gifts. We went to lunch. We even stopped for drinks in the evening before heading home.

My lifelong friends Layla and Brooklyn might have moved out of Seattle, but I'd rebound from that. People rebounded from absent friendships all the time. They filled their lives with other things, new experiences and new companions.

The companions didn't even have to be people.

I liked cats. I especially liked kittens. I'd heard once that kittens should be adopted in pairs, littermates if you could get them. That way, they kept themselves company when you were away.

A librarian with two cats.

Perfect.

Exactly how I hoped my life would end up.

I was at the Harbor Tennis Club in downtown Seattle contemplating the latest text message from Sophie Crush, the fourth close friend in our circle. Several games were underway on the indoor courts below me. The frequent sound of balls popping hollowly against the painted surface faded into the background while my herbal tea cooled on a round polished beech wood table in the lounge.

I liked herbal tea. It was a comfort drink, and I didn't want to give it up. All the same, I was thinking I might have to choose between tea and cats to keep from becoming a cliché.

I had acquaintances here at the Harbor Club, too. I'd been a member since I was a teenager. I'd taken lessons and played matches over the years with most of the other members in my age range.

But acquaintances weren't close friends. They weren't the people you could call up to spend a lazy Saturday afternoon with dressed in yoga pants, eating gourmet ice cream and loaded nachos, adding wine as soon as the clocked ticked over to four o'clock. They weren't the people you could count on when you were feeling down.

I was feeling down.

I told myself it was normal. And it was. I didn't begrudge Layla and Brooklyn their happily-ever-afters. I was happy for them. But it was hard to be happy for me right now.

I checked my cell phone screen again. The text from Sophie stared back at me.

Her lunch was running late—her lunch with her new guy was running late.

I surmised from the grinning emoji that lunch with the new guy was going great.

I was happy for her, too. Again, just not for me.

She'd canceled our Saturday tennis game at the last minute, so here I was sitting alone in my tennis shorts, my racket by my side, with no plans for the afternoon and none for the evening, either. I found myself wondering how late the animal shelter was open on weekends.

It felt pathetic again, the cat thing. I did like cats. What I didn't like was what they represented, like I'd given up and started that long, long journey through stoic mediocrity to… I don't know…retirement or death.

Wow.

I tried to laugh at myself. I'd just gone from a canceled tennis date to death in under thirty minutes. Maybe I needed tequila instead of tea.

One of the games below me ended. Two men shook hands and walked off the court.

I recognized James Gillen—Layla Kendrick's, née Gillen's, older brother. If I had to say, he was the one person in the club worse off than me.

I didn't know if that made me feel worse or better. Better for me, I suppose, since I'm human and not a saint. But worse for him—I definitely felt worse for him. Again, since I was human and capable of empathy.

I wouldn't wish his life on anyone.

James had been high-school sweethearts with my gorgeous and much sought-after friend Brooklyn. And up until this July, they'd been blissfully engaged.

They'd spent a full year planning one of the greatest weddings in the history of weddings. It would have been magnificent. In fact, it was magnificent—at least at the start, right up to the moment Brooklyn left James at the altar in front of five hundred guests and a stringer for the local newspaper.

I didn't blame Brooklyn, at least not completely. By all accounts her handsome, successful new husband, Colton Kendrick, was a real catch.

It hadn't surprised me at all that Brooklyn would have two great guys competing to marry her. Brooklyn sparkled. She always had, and I expected she always would. And that sparkle drew men—flies to honey and all that. It was a gift.

I wished I had that gift.

I pretended for a second that I did. I gave a Brooklyn-esque smile at my faint reflection in the tennis court viewing window. I tried to toss my hair the way she did, but it was fastened back in a tight braid, so my toss didn't work out.

I gave a real smile then, a laughing-at-myself smile. I took a sip of the lukewarm tea, wishing it really was tequila.

Librarians didn't sparkle. We weren't supposed to sparkle. We were practical and dependable, admirable qualities for sure. But there were no flies coming to my honey.

I removed my sports glasses and reached for my everyday pair as a couple strolled into the lounge. With my glasses back in place, I recognized them. My besieged heart sank another big notch.

It was Henry Reginald Paulson III with his pretty, bubbly girlfriend clinging to his arm.

She was tall, thin and blonde, with shiny white teeth and luscious eyelashes that seemed to blink too often. I thought her name was Kaylee or Candi or something. I'd never seen her play tennis, but nobody cared about her tennis skills. Athletic ability was obviously not on the top of Henry's wish list for a girlfriend.

The Paulson family, with Henry's parents at the center, practically ran the Harbor Club, hosting fund-raisers and sitting on the board. They were third- and fourth-generation members of the private club. Henry was the crown prince.

He was also my ex. He'd unceremoniously dumped me back in May, May 25 to be exact. It was the same day the Northridge Library had celebrated my fifth anniversary as an employee. It meant I was entitled to an extra week's holiday leave, and I moved up to parking lot B—two blocks closer to the civic building. I'd looked forward to those perks, and I'd been excited to meet Henry to cap off the day.

But our celebratory dinner at the Tidal Rush Restaurant turned into a lonely cab ride home in my blue crepe dress before the appetizers had even been served. I'd tossed the Northridge plaque into my bottom drawer and left it there.

Henry had said that night we'd stay friends. He told me I had many good qualities. He said he admired me and that one day I was going to make some man very happy.

He hadn't complained about my plain brown hair, my glasses, my understated wardrobe or my modest height. But since he'd replaced me with my physical and stylistic opposite, I could draw my own conclusions.

Henry spotted me from across the lounge.

He smiled and waved as if we had, in fact, remained friends. We hadn't even spoken since the breakup.

I wished I wasn't sitting alone right now.

I wished I was out on the court playing tennis with Sophie.

I wished I was anywhere or anything but—

"Hi, Nat." It was a man's voice directly beside my table.

I looked up to see James.

Thank you, James.

If James would only stand still and chat for a minute or two, then I wouldn't have to look completely pathetic while Henry and Kaylee joined a boisterous clique of members at a central table.

"Hi, James," I said.

"Waiting for someone?" he asked, with a glance around the expansive room.

I lifted my phone as evidence. "Sophie just canceled. I'll have to give up our court time."

"Is she okay?"

"She's fine. Something came up." Something better than me.

"Mind if I sit down?"

"No, please." I pointed to one of the other chairs at the table for four. I honestly could have kissed him right there and then.

"I'm dying of thirst," he said. He signaled to the waiter and glanced at my little teapot. "You want something else?"

The waiter promptly arrived.

"A beer," James said to him. "Whichever local one you have on tap today."

Then James looked to me, raising his brows in a question.

"Sounds good," I said.

It wasn't four o'clock yet, but on a day like this, I was in.

It took him a second to get settled into his chair.

"Good game?" I asked.

"Caleb's a strong player. I got a serious workout."

James had obviously taken a quick shower. His hair was slightly damp and he'd changed into a pair of charcoal slacks and a white dress shirt with the sleeves rolled up.

He was a good-looking man, tall and fit. He didn't have Henry's flamboyance or gregariousness. He wasn't tennis-club royalty. But he'd always been respected for his playing skills.

Now…well, now he had to contend with the tactless gossip over Brooklyn running from St. Fidelis in her wedding gown. Consensus had it that James had been marrying up, and it came as no huge surprise to some that Brooklyn had dumped him for a better offer.

I could only imagine they were saying similar things about me. My relationship with Henry had only lasted a few months, but people probably assumed I was a quick fling for him, a roll in the hay, a temporary detour to the short and mousy side.

I wondered when it would stop feeling so humiliating.

I hoped James hadn't heard the worst of the Brooklyn gossip. I really didn't subscribe to the misery-loves-company school of thought. Nope, the fewer people in the world who felt the way I did right now, the better.

"I might have to do some biking later to make up for the lost game," I said, switching my thoughts to something more productive.

I wasn't a fitness freak by any stretch, but I did count on my Saturday tennis games for a weekly workout.

"Where do you ride?" he asked.

"Along the Cadman lakeshore, mostly. My apartment's only a few blocks from Green Gardens."

"I've ridden there," he said. "It's nice in the fall."

The waiter arrived with two frosty mugs of beer.

"Can you cancel Ms. Remington's court time?" James asked as the waiter put coasters under the mugs.

"Certainly, sir."

I thanked them both with a smile. Then I gripped the handle of the generous mug. "It might not be a very long bike ride after I finish this."

James smiled at my joke and held his own beer in a toast.

I bargained with myself out loud. "Maybe I'll go tomorrow morning instead."

Then as I clinked my glass to his, I caught sight of Henry, his arm around Kaylee as he regaled the four other people at their table with some kind of a story.

"Something wrong?" James asked me.

I realized I was frowning. "No. Nothing." I turned my attention back to James.

But he looked over his shoulder and saw Henry.

"Ahhh, Paulson. That's got to be aggravating."

Aggravating wasn't exactly the word I'd use.

"It is," I said.

James's dark blue eyes turned sympathetic.

I didn't want his pity. And I didn't want him to think I was wallowing in my own misery, either—even though I was. To be fair, I was wallowing in more than just my breakup with Henry. I liked to think I'd made a bit of progress from the breakup. But on aggregate, there was a lot to wallow in about my life right now.

I tried to shake it off. "It's nothing compared to you."

The words were out before I realized how they were going to sound. I'd managed to be both tactless and insensitive all in one fell swoop. I tried to backtrack. "I mean… I didn't… I'm sorry."

"I'd rather you blurted it out than silently thought it—or whispered it like everybody else around here." He scanned the room. "And it *is* nothing compared to me. I was dumped on a much grander scale, an epic scale, the scale to end all scales here at the Harbor Club."

I wanted to disagree. I should probably disagree. But he was right, and if I said anything other than that, I'd be lying.

"How are you holding up?" I asked in a quieter tone.

"It's weird," he said. Then he took another drink. "I keep finding her stuff in my apartment. I don't know what to do with it. Do I send it to her? Do I store it for her? Do I burn it?"

"Burn it." The words had popped out. "Wait, I shouldn't have said that."

But James chuckled. "I like your style."

Brooklyn was my close friend. But even close friends did bad things. And James deserved to be angry with Brooklyn. He deserved to light something on fire.

"Then can you explain your gender to me?" I asked James.

Somehow one beer had turned into two.

"I doubt it," he said.

"Are they just shallow?"

"Mostly."

"I mean, look at Candi over there."

"I think her name is Callie."

"Not Kaylee?"

"Should we ask?"

"No!"

James chuckled at my panicked-sounding tone. I wasn't really panicked. I was just…well, self-conscious about even caring who Henry-the-cad was dating now.

I lowered my voice and leaned in. "Is she really what all men want?"

James slid a surreptitious glance to their table. "Some do."

"Some or most?"

"Okay, lots."

I heaved a sigh. I wasn't exactly disappointed, since I'd known the answer all along. Still, it didn't renew my faith in men in any way.

"Women are no better," James said.

"We're not obsessed with looks."

"You're pretty obsessed with looks, but you're even more obsessed with power and prestige."

I couldn't completely disagree. "We also want compassion and a sense of humor."

"A sense of humor is pretty hard to quantify."

"I suppose. And you can't exactly see it coming from across the room."

James tapped his mug on the table as if for emphasis. "See? Women are just like men. It's human nature to start with looks. Maybe it's because they're the easiest benchmark when you first meet."

"I wish I had them." The minute I made the admission, I wanted to call it back.

James wasn't my best friend, and this wasn't a heart-to-heart Saturday afternoon talk in yoga pants.

Now he was scrutinizing me, and I wished the floor would open right up and swallow me whole.

"Why do you say that?" he asked.

The answer was painfully obvious. "Because it *would* be nice. You must get it. You were with Brooklyn all those years."

Anybody who fell for Brooklyn understood the appeal of a beautiful woman.

"I mean, why do you think you don't have them?"

It was my turn to stare back at him.

"Hello?" I said. I pointed to my chin. "Plain Jane librarian here."

"Well, you're not exactly glamorous," he said.

"Thank you for making my point." I tamped down the ego pinch. I hadn't really expected James to insist I was beautiful. Still, blunt honesty was hard to take sometimes.

"But you're pretty."

I shook my head. "Oh, no. You can't backpedal now. Your first reaction is your true reaction."

"My first reaction was that you have the raw material."

"Be still my beating heart."

He grinned at me.

I had been joking. Well, I was mostly joking. I could

make light of my looks or I could get depressed about them. I wasn't going to get depressed.

Plain was fine. It was ordinary and normal, and people led perfectly happy lives with plain looks. In fact, most did—the vast, overwhelming majority of people had looks that were plain in some way or another. The bombshells among us were few and far between.

"You did get a look at the guy Brooklyn married, right?" James asked.

I definitely got a look at him. I hadn't attended Brooklyn's wedding to Colton Kendrick, but I'd gone to Layla's wedding right after when she married Colton's twin brother, Max. Colton and Max were rich, rugged and handsome. They also seemed to be truly great guys.

I nodded to James.

He made a sweeping gesture down his chest. "Then you can guess how I feel."

"You have the raw material," I said.

I tried not to smile. I knew heartbreak wasn't funny.

James shook his head and seemed to fight his own smile. "Are we going to sit here and wallow in it?"

"That's the opposite of what I want to do," I said.

"What do you want to do?" he asked.

I gave my racket a pointed look. "I wanted to play tennis."

"Not this minute. I mean more broadly, in life, going forward?"

"I was thinking about getting a cat."

"Seriously?"

"No. Not really."

"A cat's a big commitment."

"You don't like cats?"

He seemed to ponder the question. "I'd probably go for a dog. But I'd have to get a house first."

I knew he and Brooklyn had planned to go house shopping right after the wedding. I wasn't going to touch that one.

"A dog does need a yard," I said instead.

"Maybe I'll buy a house," he said. But he didn't look enthusiastic about it.

I wished I could afford a house. It would be years before I had a down payment saved up for even a condo. I'd be staying in my loft apartment for the foreseeable future.

"Real estate is a good investment," I said.

James was an economist. I didn't exactly know what he did on a day-to-day basis in his job, but it seemed to me economists would be interested in good investments.

"It's definitely a good time to lock in an interest rate."

"But?" I could hear the *but* in his sentence.

"It's hard to know what to look for when you can't picture your future."

The statement seemed particularly sad.

While I searched for the right response, my phone rang.

"Go ahead," James said, lifting his beer and sitting back in his chair.

"It's Sophie." I was curious about her lunch date, but I wasn't about to have an in-depth conversation here in front of James. I swiped to accept the call. "I'll tell her I'll call her back."

"You want privacy?" He made to leave.

"No." I shook my head. I didn't want to chase him away. "It's fine."

"Hi, Sophie," I said into the phone.

"Bryce has a friend," she said.

"Uh...that's nice. Listen, can I call you—"

"As in *a friend*," she said. She was talking fast, enthusiasm lighting her voice. "A friend for you, a guy who wants to meet you. We can go on a double date. Dinner tonight. Does tonight work for you?"

I found myself meeting James's gaze.

"Nat?" Sophie asked. "Are you there?"

"Yes, I'm here."

I didn't know why I was hesitating. No, I didn't have plans for Saturday night, and of course I wanted to meet a new guy. What single girl wouldn't want to meet a new guy?

It seemed like Bryce and Sophie were hitting it off. I knew Sophie had good taste in men. If Bryce was a good guy, it stood to reason that his friend would be a good guy. I'd like to meet a good guy.

"What time?" I asked.

"Seven. We'll swing by your place. You might want to meet us downstairs. I mean…you know…"

Sophie was not a fan of my utilitarian loft apartment. She bugged me about fixing it up all the time.

Myself, I didn't see the point in spending a lot of money on cosmetics. The place was perfectly functional. Then again, if the guy thought like her, I didn't want to put him off straightaway because of my questionable taste in decorating.

"Sure," I said. "Seven o'clock downstairs."

"Perfect!" She sounded really happy.

I ended the call.

"Sorry about that," I said.

James waved away my apology. "Girls' night out?"

"Not exactly. Double date."

James sat forward again. "Blind date?"

"Yes." I took a sip of my beer "I haven't been on one of those in a while."

"I guess your dry spell is over."

I didn't particularly like calling it a dry spell. It made me sound desperate—like I was thirsty for a man.

All I really wanted was to move completely and permanently on from Henry. I supposed that made me thirsty enough. There wasn't much point in dressing it up.

"That's one way to put it," I said to James.

He lifted his mug in another toast. "Well, congratulations."

I touched my mug to his again and laughed at myself. I'd just been moaning about my loneliness. I should be thrilled about having plans for tonight. I would be thrilled. I was thrilled.

"That's better," James said. "Smile and be happy."

Two

Since I hadn't thought to ask Sophie where we were going for dinner, I went middle of the road on an outfit—a pair of gray slacks and a monochrome animal print blouse. The blouse was V-necked, with long sleeves, and the rayon fabric was loose and comfortable. I liked the way it draped over my hips, asymmetrical from front to back.

I put my hair into a loose braid with a long tassel. My hair grew fast, and it had been a while since my last trim. If I left it completely loose, it felt wayward and messy, making it hard to relax while I ate. This way, it was up out of the way but still wispy around my face, so I didn't look too severe.

I wore a little more makeup than usual—though it was always disappointing when the carefully applied mascara got lost behind my glasses. I put in some dangling gold earrings Layla had given me for my last birthday, and went with a pair of medium heel, charcoal boots.

I threw a sweater over my arm since September weather was unpredictable, and I hooked my trusty brown leather tote over my shoulder. It was heavy. I often thought I should streamline the contents. But the truth was I liked to be prepared—wallet, keys, sunglasses, comb, lotion, tissues and wipes, hair elastics in case of unexpected wind, a couple of coins in each denomination, enough hidden cash for a taxi home within a twenty-five-mile radius, credit cards, my phone, a flash drive—because, well, these days you never knew when you might need to unexpectedly download data—and self-defense spray because, well, these days you just never knew.

When I met Sophie at the street entrance, I rethought my look. Then again, I usually rethought my look as soon as I saw how Sophie had dressed.

She was wearing a short black scooped-neck A-line dress with just enough swish to make it fun. Over top, she'd put a faded jean jacket with a few scattered rhinestones on the collar and shoulders. The sparkling gems echoed her choker and earrings. She carried a little clutch purse, and wore strappy black platform sandals.

Her highlighted light brown hair was thick and lustrous, framing her dark brown eyes and full lips.

"Hi, Nat," she said. "You look terrific."

I didn't feel terrific. Then again, I hadn't been going for terrific. So, there was that.

"You look fantastic," I said.

She linked her arm with mine. "Bryce is a super good guy. He got us a sedan instead of a taxi. Classy or what?"

"Classy," I said. "Where are we going?"

"Russo's on the waterfront."

"Nice," I said. Russo's was a very trendy Italian restaurant. "Do we have reservations?" Saturday nights were crowded everywhere downtown.

"You don't need to worry about that. Bryce can worry about that."

"So, you don't know if he made them or not." I wasn't being obsessive, merely practical.

"We're on a *date*, Nat. Let the guys do the planning."

"Okay." I was still curious, but I wasn't going to belabor the point.

Two men were standing in front of a black sedan parked at the curb.

"This is Bryce," Sophie said of the taller one.

Bryce was easily over six feet. His hair was thick and near jet-black. He had a classically handsome face with brown eyes and a nice smile. His shoulders were square beneath a sport jacket and a white shirt.

"Bryce is head chef at The Blue Fern," Sophie said.

"I didn't know you worked together," I said to Sophie.

She supervised food and beverage service at the local high-end restaurant. I'd had the impression Bryce was a customer she'd met while working.

"I'm sure I told you," Sophie said.

She hadn't. But I decided disputing her memory was pointless.

"Nice to meet you," I said to Bryce, offering to shake hands.

His grip was gentle, his hand broad. "Sophie talks a lot about you to me, but obviously not the other way around."

I couldn't tell if he was offended or not. I decided to take countermeasures just in case. "Our jobs are so different we really don't talk about work very much."

"Nice save," Bryce said, telling me he'd been at least slightly offended.

Sophie and I really didn't talk much about our work. But belaboring the point would only make things worse. I stopped talking.

"And this is Ethan," Sophie said, gesturing to the other man.

If she noticed she'd offended Bryce, she didn't seem particularly worried about it.

Ethan was shorter than Bryce, about Sophie's height in her high-heeled shoes—still a good bit taller than me.

His hair was a sandy blond with a copper hue. His face was on the round side, his eyes a pale blue.

"Nice to meet you too, Ethan," I said, giving him my best smile, since he was my date, and since a woman never knew when she might meet "the one." I tried to imagine Ethan as "the one." I wasn't quite seeing it, but the evening was young.

"Hi, Nat." His grip was firmer than Bryce's.

His mouth was shaped in a smile, but his eyes didn't quite seem to meet mine—odd. It looked like he was focused on my eyebrows.

It made me wonder when I'd last plucked them. Did they look messy? Bushy? I sure hoped those little blond hairs hadn't grown out in between them. That would be embarrassing.

"Do you work at The Blue Fern, too?" I asked him.

"Ethan is a computer engineer," Sophie said. "He has his own business."

"That's impressive," I said.

I'd never been strong in science and technology. Layla had always been the brainy one of the group.

"Our focus is robotics," Ethan said.

"He's a genius," Sophie said.

Ethan gave Sophie a warm smile at the compliment. "The team turns big ideas into reality. And Bryce and Sophie have presented some very exciting concepts."

I didn't understand, so I looked to Sophie for an explanation.

"We're technologically revolutionizing the food service industry," she said with a wide grin.

The way she said it sounded like she was joking, though I didn't completely get what was funny about a technological revolution of the food industry. In my mind I pictured robotic salad tossing.

The image was a little bit funny, so I smiled back at her. "You're turning The Blue Fern into *The Jetsons*? Jet packs and robot waiters?"

Their silence told me I'd got it wrong.

"You're mocking her?" Ethan asked.

I sobered. "No. I didn't... I mean..."

"It's a brave new world," Sophie said, clearly disappointed by my reaction. "You have to progress with the times."

I felt terrible.

"We should get going," Ethan said, his expression telling me I hadn't made a good first impression. So much for judging him. He was judging me.

If Sophie was serious about orchestrating a technological revolution, you'd think she might have mentioned it to her best friend.

Ethan took the front passenger seat while Sophie climbed into the back and pushed to the middle. Bryce made to climb in behind her, so I went around to the opposite door, feeling awkward and self-conscious.

"Bryce and Ethan went to high school together," Sophie said to me while I wrangled my seat belt into the clasp.

"You've been friends all this time?" I was happy to have the conversation move along.

"We weren't friends," Bryce said.

"Oh." I left it at that.

I decided to keep my responses short and sweet from here on in.

"Ethan was a nerd. I was more of a jock," Bryce said. "He went off to university, and I went to culinary school."

"You must have done well," I said. "I mean, if you're a head chef already."

"It's a small place," Bryce said.

"But we have really big plans," Sophie said.

"It sounds like," I said, leaving her an opening to elaborate.

"You've heard about 3-D printing?" she asked me.

I nodded. I didn't know a whole lot about it, library materials not normally being 3-D. Our printers were 2-D. We had color for a price, but that was as high-tech as we got.

The excitement level in Sophie's voice grew as she spoke. "The three of us are partnering on a tech start-up."

"Our patents are pending," Bryce said.

Patents?

"We've got a prototype," Ethan said from the front seat.

"You should see it, Nat," Sophie said.

"It's too big," Bryce said.

"I have some ideas on that," Ethan said.

"But you can't fault the quality," Bryce said.

"We'll need investors," Sophie said. "We need to scale up."

"Once it's perfected," Bryce said.

"We're very close," Ethan said.

I had about a thousand questions for her, starting with: *What the heck?*

"How long have you been at this?" I asked instead.

"A few months," Sophie replied. "I didn't want to jinx it, so I've kept really quiet."

"Even from me?" I felt even more isolated than I had this morning.

It looked like Bryce wasn't such a new guy in Sophie's life, after all. I felt like I was at a business meeting instead of on a date.

"I did," Sophie said. "Sorry about that."

"Just so I'm clear," I said. "You are dating Bryce?"

Bryce threaded his arm through Sophie's. "We started

off as colleagues, then friends, and now, well…we've discovered something very special."

"And Ethan brought the tech side," Sophie said.

I assumed Ethan brought the tech side to the business venture and not to the romantic relationship.

"Baker's confectionary is our domain," Ethan piped in. "We're upping the level of precision and sophistication with which restaurants, even small establishments, can conceive, refine, create and serve desserts of every variety."

"You're 3-D printing desserts?" I wasn't exactly wrapping my head around that.

I'd seen a news report once on 3-D printing action figures. They took a scan of a person's face, cartooned it, and created a personalized action figure.

I got how a printer could squirt colored plastic in a specific pattern. I wasn't seeing how it baked a cake.

"We couldn't even be thinking about this without Ethan," Sophie said. "Bryce brings the culinary expertise, and I'm bringing the business know-how. We're an awesome team."

She reached forward and squeezed Ethan's shoulder. He put his hand over hers for a second.

"So, like cakes and pies?" I asked, still skeptical.

"Oh, so much more than that," Ethan said.

"You should see how beautiful they are." Sophie smiled and sat back.

"And delicious," Bryce added, looping his arm around her shoulders. "You can build in a level of precision for incredible consistency."

Sophie nodded, looking excited. I was happy for her. She'd always had boundless energy and enthusiasm, and an impressive sense of adventure. Growing up, it was always Sophie who came up with the ideas for our adventures.

It seemed she'd gotten bored at work—but in a good way. She was branching out to a brand-new venture, and it even came with a romance.

The driver pulled to a stop at the curb and I shifted my attention to Russo's front patio. It was a lovely building, decorated with tiny white lights on clusters of potted trees. The walkway and stairs were red cobblestones, and the front door was made of thick oak planks with gold embossed hinges and handles.

Bryce opened the car door and stepped out and turned to help Sophie.

I went out my side and walked over the uneven cobblestones around the back of the car, glad for the moment that I'd gone with sturdy boots.

In her spike high heels, Sophie hung on to Bryce's arm. Ethan and I fell in behind them.

I felt awkward walking silently beside Ethan.

"You grew up in Seattle?" I asked to break the ice.

"I was three when we moved out from Boston."

"I was born here," I said, keeping the conversational ball rolling. "We lived in Queen Anne."

"Wallingford. My parents are university faculty members."

"His mom's a renowned chemistry professor," Sophie said over her shoulder.

Bryce opened the big door and we all walked into the dim interior of Russo's.

"That's very impressive," I said to Ethan.

"Professor Mary Quinn." He sounded quite proud. "She's published over thirty articles in technical journals. Perhaps you've read some of them?"

I didn't have an immediate response. I wasn't sure why he thought I'd be reading chemistry articles.

"Since you're a librarian," he prompted.

"I'm in the public library. We don't catalog many scientific journals."

He seemed surprised by that. "Really? Have you considered the importance of STEM to young readers? And, really, to any readers?" He took a beat. "STEM stands for science, technology, engineering and mathematics."

I knew what STEM stood for. "It's a matter of capacity. For technical works, I'd refer people to the university library, or maybe the State Association of Chemists."

We'd stopped in front of the reception desk.

"Do you have a reservation?" the hostess asked Bryce.

"Brookside for four," Bryce said.

Sophie turned to us, a little sigh in her voice. "I wish I was that smart."

"You are smart," I said to her.

She had a business degree. She was only twenty-six, and she was already a manager at one of the best boutique restaurants in the city.

"I'm not science smart."

"You're real-world smart, and that's much more practical."

Silence followed my words.

Again.

"There's nothing more practical than science," Ethan said.

"It takes a team," Bryce said.

Ethan kept talking. "Science is responsible for everything from advanced agriculture to green mining techniques to fabric dyes for fashion shows, and all the obvious technologies. Take your cell phone, for instance. It took generations of highly trained scientists to develop the concepts that make a smartphone run."

"And we're grateful for that," Bryce put in.

"Right this way," the hostess said to us.

"I do enjoy my cell phone." I took Bryce's lead and tried to lighten the conversation.

Bryce followed the hostess. Sophie went behind him as we wound our way through the tables.

I took up the rear.

The friendly woman showed us to a booth with a half-circle bench. It was on the second floor overlooking the harbor. After a bit of fumbling over the seating arrangements, I ended up on one end of the bench next to Ethan. Bryce took the other end, and Sophie was sandwiched between the two men.

"Drinks?" Bryce asked, opening the cocktail menu.

"Oh, a cranberry martini for me," Sophie said.

"I'll take one of those," Ethan said.

"I'm having a Canadian whiskey," Bryce said, looking to me.

"A glass of cabernet sauvignon," I said.

A glass now and a glass with dinner, I decided. Then I'd be nicely relaxed.

"This whole thing started when we lost our pastry chef," Sophie said. "And we were having trouble finding a new one with the skills and expertise."

"The ante keeps going up and up," Bryce said.

"Enter technology," Ethan said.

"I did an informal poll of our customers," Sophie explained. "And dessert was the number one determiner of restaurant choice among women. It was only number three for men. They like steak and seafood."

Ethan jumped back in. "Studies show that on a date, especially the first few dates, men go where women want to go."

"And the business world is drastically changing," Sophie said. "There are more women executives."

"They want great dessert on their expense accounts," Ethan said.

"Studies show?" I asked him.

"That's just logic," he said.

"The skill level, the prep area, the prep time," Bryce listed off on his fingers. "There's a reason most restaurants have limited dessert menus, especially the small establishments."

"We knew technology could help," Ethan said. "Hence, the inception of BRT Innovations."

"Our company," Sophie said, pointing to all three of them.

"I see." I didn't see everything yet. But I had a feeling I was going to learn a whole lot more before the night was through.

As a date, the evening hadn't gone particularly well. As a business meeting, it had gone quite a bit better.

I hadn't exactly kept up, but I'd learned how much time, thought and energy had gone into the idea for Sweet Tech. If everything they said came to fruition, my friend Sophie really was going to technologically revolutionize desserts.

They'd dropped me off at ten thirty.

Ethan had dutifully walked me to the lobby door. He hadn't kissed me, just said good-night and that he'd had a nice time.

I said I'd had a nice time, too. I suspected our level of enthusiasm for each other was about equal.

On the upside, the restaurant had been lovely, the food delicious.

I'd had the grilled sole with a spring greens salad, opting for a brandy instead of dessert. A good decision since, on top of the wine, it had lulled me into a lovely deep sleep.

I felt rested this morning, ready for my bike ride along the lakeshore.

No more jealousy over Sophie's adventure, I decided. No more moaning about being stood up for yesterday's tennis game. I felt like an independent woman in the morning sunshine, pedaling along the paved bike path, up little rises and down small hills, the wind whistling past my ears.

"Good on you." A voice came up on my left side.

I looked sideways and realized my glasses were sliding down my nose.

I pushed them into place and saw James coming up to pedal alongside me.

"I wasn't sure if you were serious," he said.

"I was serious. I like bike riding."

"I can see that."

I smiled. I was happy to see him. We'd joked quite a lot yesterday, and I'd had fun.

"I prefer rowing," he said.

I knew he'd been on a championship team in college. "Yet, here you are."

"Here I am. You inspired me."

The idea of inspiring James amused me. "Like your own personal trainer? 'Get your butt out of that bed, Gillen! Gear up! Outside! Give me twenty!'"

James laughed at my imitation of a drill sergeant. "Twenty laps of the lake? That seems a bit ambitious."

"We probably should have packed a lunch," I said, feeling lighthearted in the fresh air and sunshine.

A woman and two children approached us riding the other way, a boy and a girl looking about ten years old. The kids had flushed cheeks and windblown hair and were pedaling hard to keep up with their mother.

James shifted in behind me to give them space to pass. We both stayed tight to the right side of the path.

"How was your date?" he asked after the family passed.

A man was throwing a ball for his dog on the grass beside us, and I kept a watch in front of me as the animal ran close to the path.

"It was fine," I answered.

"Fine as in good, or fine as in meh?"

"Fine as in…mediocre, I guess." Sophie's business plans were secret for now, so I wasn't going to talk about them.

It would have been nice if the date part had gone better. I'd wanted to like Ethan. I mean, he wasn't that bad. Other women might like him just fine.

"Sorry to hear that," James said. "Where did you go?"

"Russo's."

"That sounds nice. Did you have the prime rib?"

"The grilled sole."

"Their prime rib is to die for."

"I'll try that next time."

"Is there going to be a next time?"

"I hope so." Then I realized he meant a next date. "I don't know about a next date. But I'll definitely go back to Russo's."

"Nix the guy, stick with the restaurant. I do like your style, Nat."

"The guy seemed fine." I felt guilty dissing him. "His name was Ethan. He's a tech guy. He seems very smart."

"But no second date? Are you one of those picky women with a long list of qualities you want in a man?"

"What? No. I'm not like that. I don't have a list."

At least, I didn't have one that was written down. But I'd admit there were certain things I was looking for—a sense of humor, for example, a progressive world-view, maybe somewhat more humble than Ethan. And I wouldn't be wild about someone who smoked or drank to excess or who, say, had a gambling addiction.

"You're listing it off now," James said with a tone of amazement.

"I'm not…" But I was.

He'd caught me.

"It's not a long list," I said defensively.

"What's on it?"

"What's on yours?" I asked.

"Are you thirsty?" he asked.

We were coming to a snack bar near a sandy beach and a play area.

"Are you changing the subject?" I asked.

"No, I'm just thirsty."

"Okay. I'll take a sparkling water. But then I want to hear what's on your list."

We both slowed our bikes, coasting to the dark green bike rack set next to a scattered group of picnic tables.

I pushed my bike tire between two bars.

"Spill," I said, smoothing my windblown hair.

I'd pulled it back into a ponytail, but some strands had come loose around my face. I tried not to imagine what I looked like. Some women looked cute when they were all disheveled. I looked messy. On me, messy wasn't cute or sexy or anything other than messy.

"It's a short list," he said, dismounting.

"That should make it easy."

"Not Brooklyn."

I felt a lurch of guilt. I probably should have kept my big mouth shut about relationships. James didn't need this on a leisurely Sunday morning bike ride. I felt terrible.

"Now you give me something," he said.

He didn't sound sad or upset.

I was grateful for that. Maybe I hadn't completely spoiled the morning.

"No gambling addiction," I said.

"Seriously?" he asked as we walked to the counter. "You felt the need to include that on a list?"

"You think I should date a guy with a gambling addiction?" I asked.

The teenage girl behind the counter gave us an odd look.

I thought about clarifying the statement, but it seemed silly to launch into an explanation for a stranger whose life would only intersect with mine for a matter of minutes.

"Two Sparkletts," James said to her. "Plain."

The teenager turned and moved to the cooler.

"I don't think you should date a serial killer, either," he said to me. "But you don't need to put that on a list anywhere. It's obvious."

"I'd rather date an addicted gambler than a serial killer."

The teenager heard that one too, and gave us another puzzled look. "That'll be seven fifty."

James handed her a ten. "No need for change. Thanks."

"Thank you," she said with an appreciative smile.

We each took one of the bottles. I couldn't help but wonder what the clerk thought as we walked away.

"That girl back there thinks I'm dating a gambling addict," I said, twisting off the bottle cap.

"She really doesn't care."

"I suppose not. Still, I hope I didn't accidently set a bad example."

"I think you're safe." James took a long drink. "Now, give me a real one."

"A real what."

"A real item on your list."

I wanted to tell him to give me a real item, too. I didn't think "not Brooklyn" was legitimate. But I didn't want to risk upsetting him.

"Good sense of humor," I said.

"Too generic," he said.

"It's legitimate."

"What else?"

"A progressive worldview."

"What does that mean?"

"It means you're progressive." I kept my expression deadpan. "You know, in your worldview."

James grinned. "Touché."

"You give me one."

"Me? But I'm a sad sack recovering from utter heartbreak."

I took in his überinnocent expression. "I *knew* that was a ruse." I shoved him with my upper arm.

"Not buying it?" he asked.

"Dish."

"Okay, let me see…hardworking."

"And you say *I'm* too generic."

"You think I should date a lazy woman?"

"Depends. Exactly how good does she look eating bonbons in front of daytime television?"

"Nobody looks good doing that."

We came to our bikes and stood there while we finished our drinks.

"I don't know what I'm looking for," I said.

"Love?" James asked.

"Now, *that's* the generic answer."

"But true." He took my empty bottle from me.

I knew he was right. "But how do you find it?"

I was serious. I felt like it had always eluded me. I mean, I'd liked Henry a lot, but with him, even when things were going well, it sure didn't feel like the poems and stories said it would.

James headed for the recycle bin. "You look really hard," he called back over his shoulder.

He tossed the bottles and started back. "Meet a lot of people, I guess. Statistically speaking, that'll give you the best shot at falling in love."

We mounted up.

"There are people everywhere," James said as we continued down the path.

He pointed to the beach. "There's one, and another, and another. Take your pick."

I chuckled as I pedaled beside him. It was silly, and it was funny, and it felt good to laugh at life.

"What about her?" I asked as we came up on a pretty woman in a white bathing suit cover-up.

"Mommy, Mommy." A two-year-old boy threw himself in her arms.

"Taken," James said.

"Either of them?" I joked about two women in their sixties chatting in matching lawn chairs.

"Wrong era," he said.

"You're so fussy."

"Him?" James nodded to a shirtless jogger with a tiny dog on a leash.

The twentysomething man's chest was shaved, and his bulging pecs were shiny with oil.

"Too self-obsessed," I said.

"You can tell that just by looking?"

"You can't? How many hours a week at the gym do you suppose that takes?"

"I guess," James said.

"When would he mow the lawn or clean the gutters, or play with the children, or plan date night?"

"You *do* have a long list."

"I'm a practical woman. It's not like I won't help around the house. But I'm not cleaning the gutters all by myself."

"I can respect that," James said.

We pedaled along in our own thoughts until we reached the far end of the lake where the path curved sharply over a wooden bridge that cut across a burbling creek.

"You want to take a rest?" James asked.

A wooden bench was positioned on a concrete pier that jutted out into the lake.

"Sure."

We pulled our bikes onto a grassy patch and took the empty bench.

"I think we're coming at this all wrong," James said.

"Coming at what?" My first thought was the bike ride. Did he not like the lakeshore path?

"It really is a numbers game."

"Riding?"

"No, meeting the opposite sex. You need to meet a lot of eligible people to up your odds."

"Sure."

Who would argue with that? Not me. I might not be a science nerd, but I understood the law of large numbers.

"And we need to bring them to us."

"The eligible people?" I wasn't exactly seeing what he meant. Were we going back to the crowded beach?

"Think about Callie."

My face pinched up. "What about her? And are you sure it's not Kaylee?"

"We can call her whatever you want."

"I always thought she looked like a Candi."

"Candi." He paused in thought. "She does sort of look like a Candi."

"Don't drool," I said.

"I didn't mean it like that."

"Yes, you did."

James grinned unrepentantly. "Okay, we both agree most men would point at her from across the room."

"We do."

He was right. Candi was gorgeous and glamorous and eminently desirable.

"And we agree that most women would point at the Kendrick twins from across the room."

I was surprised he brought them up. "Yes."

Separate or together Colton and Max Kendrick were definitely pointworthy.

"Let's do that," James said.

I was really puzzled now. "Point at people from across the room?"

"No." James shook his head. "Get people to point at us."

Three

"Explain to me again how this works?" I said to James.

We'd finished our ride, locked up our bikes, and found ourselves a table on a deck overlooking the Orchid Club courtyard at the edge of the park.

"The view is perfect," James said. "Are you ready to take notes?"

"I can take notes." I had my phone. It had apps.

He glanced at his watch. "There'll be an event at the club tonight."

"What's the event?"

A waiter came by with a platter of nachos and two beers with quarters of lime stuck in the necks of the bottles. I'd also been eyeing the mini éclairs pictured on the menu. But I'd decide on that later. I was holding out hope the nachos would fill me up enough to take the éclairs off my mind.

"I don't know the event," James said. "It doesn't matter. Whatever it is, it'll be posh. People will be dressed up, looking fine. We're going to pick out our favorites."

"Please tell me we're not going to talk to them."

I was still wearing my yoga pants and an oversize

T-shirt. And I was still slightly damp with sweat. The sun was going down, and I was grateful for the propane heater stationed next to our table.

"Were you not paying attention?" James asked, looking stern.

I looked to the club entrance. "Did I miss something?"

"*We're* not approaching them. *They're* going to approach us."

"Dressed like *this*?" I gestured to my chest.

"Not these people. Other people. Future people. Tonight, we pick out the pointworthy people and take notes on what makes them pointworthy. Then, we replicate it."

"What if it's genetics? I'm not getting plastic surgery."

A new hairstyle and a fancy dress were only going to get me so far. It's not like I'd never dressed up before. I'd dressed up plenty of times. Dressing up didn't turn me into Brooklyn or Sophie or anyone else.

James was giving me a horrified look. "Who said anything about plastic surgery?"

"What if we decide I need a new nose? Or..." I glanced down at my chest. "Upgraded breasts?"

"You don't need upgraded breasts!"

He gave a glance around at the other tables and moved his chair closer in, lowering his voice. "I told you, you already have the raw material."

"I'm not so sure about that. Wait. Look. There's a limo."

I pulled out my phone and hit the notes app. "Who is it?"

A man got out of the back seat.

He looked about fifty.

"Nice tux," I said.

"Formal wear gets your attention?" James asked.

"Formal wear is good, depending on the occasion. I wonder if this is a wedding."

"Could be the father of the bride," James said.

The man extended his hand and helped a middle-aged woman out of the limo.

She was followed by two younger men in business suits.

"Which one attracts your attention?" James asked. "Don't think, just blurt it out."

"The guy with dark hair."

"Why?"

"He's tall."

"I could put lifts in my shoes," James said.

"You're tall," I said to him.

"Other men are taller."

"You're tall enough."

James was well over six feet. I'd say six-two. A whole lot taller than that and the height started to be a detractor. There was a perfect sweet spot. He was in it.

"What else?" he asked me.

"His shoulders," I said. "They're broad, but it's more than that. There's something to the set of his shoulders. It makes him look confident. Confident is good."

"Confident shoulders." James flexed his.

I chuckled. "Yes. Confident shoulders."

Another vehicle pulled up. This was a big white SUV. Four girls piled out wearing identical aquamarine dresses.

"Wedding," James said.

"Definitely."

We were both silent for a moment while they settled themselves into a group.

James munched on a nacho.

"So, which one?" I asked.

"Auburn hair," he said.

"You like auburn hair?"

He shook his head. "It's not the hair color. It's… I would say the shape of her figure and the brightness of her smile."

I jotted down "bright smile."

I found myself running my tongue over my teeth. I'd whitened them a few months ago. But maybe it was time to have it professionally done. I needed a dental checkup soon. I could easily get some whitening at the same time.

It couldn't hurt.

"She has a graceful walk," James said.

"I could practice that," I said.

He looked at me. "I never paid any attention to your walk. Walk somewhere and let me look."

The request made me super self-conscious. "No."

He pointed. "Over to the exit and back."

"I'm not going to walk for you."

"How can I help you if you won't let me assess you?"

Assess me? "I'd feel ridiculous."

"Well, get the heck over that. I'm going to do whatever you want."

I couldn't let that opportunity stay hanging. "Whatever I want?"

"You know what I mean. I'll walk. I'll talk. I'll make confident shoulders. Come on, Nat. If this is going to work, we have to trust each other."

I realized he was right. Everything he'd said and done so far made me believe he was sincere. I should get over myself and take his help.

It was either that or cats, cats and tea, tea and cats until I was old and gray and alone.

I stood. "Don't you dare tell anyone about this, especially not Layla."

I'd be mortified if he told his sister that I was on a self-improvement binge.

"You think I want Layla to know what we're doing? You think I want *anyone* to know?"

"So, our secret?"

"Yes."

"To the grave?"

"You want me to pinky swear?"

"That would be good."

He solemnly held up his pinky.

I hooked mine around it, and we both broke into twin grins.

"I pinky swear," he said.

"So do I."

His hand was warm and strong, his skin rougher than mine. It felt odd to touch him, and I realized how rarely it happened.

I'd seen James hug Brooklyn countless times. He hugged Layla, of course. And I'd even seen him hug Sophie—who pulled pretty much everybody into hugs at one point or another.

James and I, on the other hand, had always kept a respectful distance.

I hadn't thought about it until now.

But now I was thinking about it.

He dropped his hand from mine.

"Walk," he said.

I turned, took a breath and walked straight to the exit. There I turned and walked back, trying really hard not to feel utterly stupid.

"More glide," he said when I got back to the table.

"What do you mean?"

"Smoother, don't clunk when you walk, and keep your feet closer together, more like you're walking on a line than on the two sides of a railroad track."

"A *railroad track*?" Just how unattractive was my walk?

"Do it again," he said.

It was on the tip of my tongue to refuse.

But I told myself to buck up. Maybe my ugly walk had

been the problem all these years. I wondered why nobody had said anything before now.

I glanced around to make sure the people at the other tables weren't paying attention. They weren't.

I breathed again, really deep this time.

I turned and walked—glided, I hoped. I pretended I was on a balance beam, moving my feet together with each step.

I turned.

I couldn't look at James.

I picked a spot in the trees above his head and I did my best to glide back.

"Hmm," he said.

Embarrassed, I sat down before he could tell me to do it again.

"Hmm?" I mimicked. "I get a hmm?"

"It was better. I think."

"You *think*?"

"You seemed a bit stiff."

"Well, of *course* I was stiff. I could feel you watching me."

"We'll practice."

"We?"

"I'll do the shoulder thing."

I looked back down at the courtyard to see that three more vehicles had arrived. "Oh, I'm going to find something way better than the shoulder thing for you to practice."

I was definitely not going to be in this alone.

"Bring it on," he said.

I watched two more couples get out of their cars.

Valets had arrived and were moving the cars away as more people turned up.

"That guy," I said to James. "The one in the blue blazer."

"You like him?" James squinted. "Next time we should bring binoculars."

"We're going to be stalkers?"

"Private eyes. Investigators. We're investigators investigating beautiful people."

"It seems a bit invasive to me."

"What do you like about blue blazer guy?"

"He looks relaxed." I gazed at James to contrast the two men. "You look uptight."

"I do?"

I nodded. "You do. You look critical, like the world isn't quite measuring up to your standards and you're about to tell it why. That guy down there, he looks like he loves the world and can't wait to meet it and have fun with it."

James gazed at the courtyard. "Interesting. I'm not sure how I practice that."

"Tequila." The suggestion jumped out of my brain.

"I'm game." He munched on another nacho. "But I'm not sure how much tequila will help with your walking problem."

I smiled and reached for a nacho myself. "Are we really going to do this?"

He met my gaze. "I think we are."

"Embark on a secret mission to make ourselves irresistible to the opposite sex?" I bit down on the nacho. It was delicious, and I was hungry.

"Law of large numbers until we fall in love."

"Okay," I said.

This was by far the oddest thing I'd ever done. But however it turned out, it was going to be way better than cats.

"You *have* to come with us." Sophie shut the heavy door of my apartment behind her.

I lived in what was once an elementary school and

had been converted to thirty apartments. I was on the third of three floors in a high-ceilinged loft under what were now murky skylights, with an aging wood floor partially covered in scattered worn rugs. The walls were gray-painted cinder blocks, enclosing a single big room, plus a bathroom.

I'd added a freestanding wooden divider to cordon off the bed. I didn't like making beds, and I didn't want the world to see my failing.

"Nat," Sophie said with an urgency to her tone.

"Did Ethan specifically ask you to invite me?" I was having a hard time believing Ethan wanted another date with me.

Sophie paced to the cluster of sofas and armchairs on one side of the room. "Of *course* he wants you to come. That's the whole point, that the four of us would have fun together again."

"I didn't think he had fun last time." I went to the kitchen area to get a pitcher of iced tea from the fridge.

"Sure he did. Didn't you?"

"I felt a little out of place." I dropped ice cubes into two glasses.

"Why?"

I turned to look at her. "Because all you talked about was the dessert project."

"We talked about other stuff."

I had to grin at that. "A little bit. But it was mostly about Sweet Tech."

"I'm sorry." She dropped down on the arm of one chair. "Are you mad at me?"

I poured the iced tea. "I'm not mad. I didn't say I was mad."

"We didn't mean to be boring. I'm sure Ethan didn't mean to be boring."

"You weren't boring." I crossed the room and handed her a glass. "You were excited. And I'm excited for you. I just don't think Ethan and I are going to work."

"You didn't really give him a chance."

"I didn't feel a spark." I sat down in my favorite burgundy armchair.

I'd moved it and the matching burgundy sofa from my parents' basement on the other side of the city. I bought my brown sofa and the two leather contour chairs from an online reseller. They all surrounded a square glass-topped coffee table.

Sophie took an end of the sofa cornerwise from mine.

"You barely had a chance to get to know him."

That might be true. But I was pretty confident in my impression.

"Did it take a long time with you and Bryce? Could you tell right away that you liked him?"

"We were always friendly," she said. Then she seemed to give it some thought. "I never disliked him. Do you dislike Ethan?"

"I don't know him well enough to dislike him."

She made a mock toast with her iced tea. "Thank you for making my point."

I sighed. I didn't feel like having this argument.

I'd only been home from work for about twenty minutes. But I'd already slipped into a loose cotton T-shirt and a pair of worn blue jeans. I was planning to make a bowl of soup, then putter around in my sundeck garden for a while. The heather was still nice, and the pansies and chrysanthemums would last a few more weeks. I wanted to enjoy my little patch of outdoors as long as the weather held.

Afterward, I was thinking I might search for a video on graceful walking. Surely, I wasn't the only woman in the world with that particular challenge. I didn't want

James to frown at me and say *hmm* the next time I tried walking for him.

"My car's out front," Sophie said. "I'll tell Bryce we're going to meet them there. That way you don't have to rush to get ready, and we can come home whenever you want."

"I wasn't planning to celebrate Technology Week," I said.

"This is a fun event. It's not nerdy at all. It's the Things Festival—phones and tablets and home alarm systems. It's stuff you should be learning about anyway. Don't you want to see the hologram exhibit?"

"I was planning to garden after dinner." I knew there was a whine in my voice, but I was feeling a little whiny at the thought of going back out again tonight.

"Come on, Nat. You can garden any old time. And it's way more fun when you're there."

Now I felt selfish. Sophie obviously liked Bryce a lot. She wanted my support, and I should buck up and give it to her.

I glanced at my torn jeans. "Do I have to change?"

"It's definitely come-as-you-are. Flats are better for walking around."

"I haven't eaten yet."

"There'll be vendors."

"With 3-D printed food?" I joked.

She looked worried. "I sure hope not. We're trying to be ahead of the curve."

"That was a joke," I said.

"Oh. Good. It'll be more like burgers and nachos."

"I can live with that," I said, forcing myself to stand up and show some enthusiasm. "Give me a minute."

Leaving Sophie to finish her iced tea, I cut past my bed to the bathroom, freshened my face and tossed my hair into a ponytail.

Then I hoisted my shoulder bag from the bed. I hesitated, testing its weight in my hand for a moment. Deciding to play the odds and be more comfortable, I stuffed the essentials into my jeans pockets—my phone, a credit card, a little bit of money, a mini comb and a couple sticks of gum.

Back in the living area, I laced up my runners and tied a sweater around my waist. "I'm ready."

"You're fast," Sophie said, coming to her feet.

"Do you have to stop and change?" I asked.

She was wearing blue jeans and heeled black boots with a burgundy tunic sweater that had a loose cowl neck and a row of oversize buttons. Her hair was airy and fluffy and framed her face.

"I'll just go like this."

Once again, she looked chic to my utilitarian.

I wasn't going to let myself worry about that. It wasn't like I wanted to impress Ethan.

I locked up and we headed down the central staircase.

My phone buzzed against my butt and I retrieved it from my pocket.

It was James.

For some reason, my chest gave a little lift at the sight of his name.

I didn't want to answer in front of Sophie, but I didn't want to not answer, either. So I slowed my steps and let her get ahead.

"Hi," I said into the phone, sounding more breathless than I'd expected.

"Are you biking?" he asked.

"Heading down the stairs."

"Doing stairs. Good for you." He sounded impressed.

"No, not *doing* stairs, just going down them. I'm with Sophie."

"Oh. I misunderstood. Girls' night out?"

"No, another double date."

There was a pause on the line. "Oh… With mediocre guy?"

I hung back even farther. "I don't think you should call him that. But, yes, with Ethan again." I listened for a second. "James?"

"I shouldn't bother you, then."

"It's no bother. We're just heading out. What's up?"

"I was thinking about the weekend. But you probably have a date."

"I don't have a date." I didn't expect to have a date. I was going along tonight to support Sophie.

I came to the bottom of the stairs as Sophie was on her way out the door.

"What were you thinking?" I asked James.

I wouldn't mind having some plans for the weekend. I wouldn't mind it at all. If nothing else, it would give me a good answer on Friday when people asked what I was doing.

"That we could shop for some new clothes. I don't know anything about the right places or the right designers, but we could look that up. We have to start somewhere."

"We do," I agreed.

I'd never gone clothes shopping with a guy before. I usually went with Sophie and Brooklyn. Which, now that I thought about it, was usually about their clothes and not mine.

I pretty much had a set style: Miles Carerra for blazers and skirts, Nordin for slacks and Mistress Hinkle for blouses. I rarely bought dresses. I stuck with my classic standbys that I'd had for a few years now.

I picked up jeans, yoga pants and T-shirts at the outlet mall. I didn't much care who made them, as long as they fit.

"So?" James prompted.

Sophie had stopped. Holding the door open, she waited, watching me with a puzzled expression.

I tried to look like I was having a business conversation. "What time?"

"I'll text Saturday morning. Around nine?"

"That'll work. I better go. Sophie's waiting."

"Have a mediocre time."

I couldn't help but smile as I started walking. "That's kind of what I'm expecting."

"Who was that?" Sophie asked. "What are you expecting?"

"I'm expecting the Things Festival to be interesting," I said.

"That's the spirit."

She didn't press me for more information on the phone call, and I didn't volunteer. The James and Nat self-improvement project was going to stay a closely guarded secret.

As we climbed into Sophie's car, my phone pinged.

I checked to see the message was from James.

Enjoying the mediocrity?

I sent a smiley face back, because he'd made me smile.

"What's going on?" Sophie asked as she pulled into traffic.

"Work," I said.

I didn't explain what kind of work. And creating a whole new me was going to take a lot of work. It was going to take a *whole* lot of work.

So I reasoned that I wasn't lying. I was misdirecting. Misdirecting wasn't exactly noble, but it wasn't the worst sin in the world, either.

And I was being Sophie's wingman tonight—reluctantly

but with good humor, I was helping a friend. I hoped the two things balanced each other out.

On Saturday morning, James picked me up in a low-slung red convertible.

It shone bright under the sunshine, looking out of place against the dusty curb.

"Is this new?" I asked, shading my eyes. My clip-on sunglasses were in my purse, and I decided I was going to need them.

As usual, I was glad to be prepared.

"I bought it yesterday," James said. "What do you think?"

I didn't know what I thought. Mostly I thought, *Holy cow!* "It's very red."

"Isn't it?"

"Yes."

"I went to the dealer at lunchtime."

"Uh-huh." I was trying to think of something positive to say.

The car was pretty ugly, low to the ground, a bit boxy. The black interior was harsh. It looked like something a gangster might have owned in the '70s. And I wasn't sure about owning a convertible in Seattle. We had plenty of nice days in the summer, I supposed. But we had plenty of rain, too. And the winters were a mixture of slush and ice. It was hard to tell how well the car would stay heated.

"I took a good look at everything they had," James said.

"And you picked this?"

"You hate it."

"I… It's… It definitely doesn't seem like something you'd pick."

"I know. That's the point. I picked the one I wouldn't

have picked. It's a *new me* car." He opened the passenger door to let me in.

"I suppose."

If we were changing who we were, I guessed what you drove was part of that.

I had a ten-year-old crossover, hunter green. It was serviceable if not beautiful. It definitely wasn't flashy.

I held on to the back of the bucket seat as I lowered myself inside. It was low, really low. If we had to hide under the trailer of a semi, we were going to fit just fine.

James shut the door, and I felt like I was sitting on the sidewalk.

He rounded the back and got in on the driver's side.

He popped a pair of sunglasses on his face and adjusted the rearview mirror.

"Do you like the way it drives?" I asked.

He started the engine, and it throbbed beneath us, roaring under the hood.

Since the top was down, I could hear every piston.

"It corners like a supercar," he said.

"I take it that's good?"

"It's very good."

"Okay," I said.

"Buckle up."

I snapped myself in.

The tires chirped as we jolted away. James wound out the engine in first, then grabbed second gear and we lurched forward.

I was sucked back against my seat.

He quickly braked, since we were coming to a red light.

"Comfortable?" he called to me above the noise and the wind.

"The seat's nice," I said.

"What?" He cupped his ear.

"The seat's nice!" I called out.

He nodded.

The light turned green and we lurched forward again. It had good acceleration, I'd give it that.

We slowed and turned onto the I-5 on-ramp, and James pressed on the gas.

We were going faster than traffic and easily merged.

Something hit me in the forehead. It stung, and I flinched.

"What?" he asked me.

I reached up to find a smashed bug on my forehead.

I held it out to him. "I'm not crazy about having the top down."

He laughed at me.

The cad.

Okay, I'd admit it was kind of funny.

"You'd think the windshield would be a little higher," he said.

Then he flinched, and I saw a black spot on his cheek. This time I laughed at him.

He geared down. He flipped on his signal and took an exit.

"This sucks," he said.

"It's a little bit funny," I said.

"This is a stupid car."

"You don't like it?" I wanted to ask if he'd even test-driven it before he bought it. It seemed like an awfully impulsive purchase.

"You hate it," he said.

"It's not about what I like."

"Okay, I hate it."

We were slowing down now, and the noise wasn't quite so oppressive.

"So why did you buy it?"

"Like I said, I didn't want to buy something I liked."

"Like a practical sedan?"

He turned onto a side street. "I've had one of those for years."

"Maybe you went too far the other way."

"Maybe."

"You know." I was thinking this through as I spoke. "We're going to have to like the people we turn into."

He turned into the empty lot of a small park. "The danger in that is that we'll stay exactly as we are. We have to expand."

"We can choose the direction we expand in."

"We can't trust our own instincts. Our own instincts are what brought us to where we are."

I had to admit, he had a point.

He brought the car to a halt in a parking spot facing a baseball diamond.

"How about this," I said. "I'll trust your instincts, and you trust mine. That way we change it up, but we don't…" I gestured to the dashboard. "We don't do something completely stupid."

"Are you calling me stupid?"

"I'm calling this car stupid. It's going to be freezing in the winter, if you don't lose it in the first snowfall. I feel like a kindergarten kid sitting down so low. The black leather looks like something a gangster would own. And it's butt ugly, James. Fire-engine red? What, are you having a midlife crisis?"

James started to laugh.

"I'm just saying…"

"The dealership's only about five miles from here."

"Can you take it back?" That seemed like the best course of action to me—the very best course of action.

"I can probably exchange it for something else."

I breathed a sigh. "I think you should."

"I think I should, too. And I think you're picking the next one."

"What?"

He couldn't be serious.

He put it in Reverse. "We've determined we can't trust my taste."

"But…I can't pick you out a car. A pair of blue jeans, sure. Maybe a tux. Maybe even a hat."

"You think I need a hat."

"No. I'm not saying you need a hat. You don't need a hat. You have very nice hair."

He did have very nice hair, thick and dark, classically cut in a way that showed off his square jaw and gorgeous blue eyes.

He headed for the parking lot exit. "You're picking the new one, Nat."

I tried to be helpful. "You just have to go…I don't know…a little less…flamboyant."

"I'm sure you will."

"I'm not doing it alone, James."

"Ah, but you are. You volunteered."

"I did not."

"And I quote—*you* trust *my* instincts."

He looked completely serious.

I considered for a moment the strategy of choosing something completely ridiculous, like a superlifted pickup truck. Then he'd have to overrule me. That could work.

"I can hear what you're thinking," he said as we tooled along a main road.

"You cannot."

"You're thinking if you botch it, I'll have to take over. I'm not going to take over. This one's on you."

"You've lost your mind."

"Nope. I've gained yours. I think I got the good end of that trade."

I couldn't help but smile. "Then are you going to pick *me* out a new car?"

He glanced over at me. "Absolutely."

I'd been joking. "I can't afford a new car."

"It doesn't have to be brand-new. But cars are like clothes. They introduce us to the world."

I gestured to the dashboard again. "And *this* is what you wanted to say?"

"I plead temporary insanity."

Four

I chose a gunmetal-gray SUV. It had sleek curves, a tough-looking black grille, diamond-shaped headlights, big durable wheels that would stand up to any weather conditions, and comfortable seats that made you feel like you were sitting on a cloud.

I didn't analyze my choice too closely. I just knew that if three men drove up, one in a sports car, one in a sedan and one in an SUV, I'd be most interested in the SUV guy.

Maybe it projected strength, or maybe there was room in the back for my eventual kids. It could easily have been anthropology and my primal brain influencing my decision. But I picked it, and James bought it, and we left a very happy salesman behind.

"This is way better," James said as we drove along I-5 and he fiddled with the controls on the dashboard.

"I can hear every word you say," I said. "It's like a miracle."

"Yeah, yeah. I get it. Your taste is better than my taste."

I felt a moment of doubt. "As long as you truly like it."

"I like it a lot." His smile turned warm and his tone was sincere.

I liked how his voice sounded in my ears. I liked how the warmth made me feel—like I'd done something right and he was happy about it.

"We're going downtown," he said. "I researched the 'it' places to buy a tux."

"You're seriously buying a tux? You can rent those, you know."

"Be honest, Nat. Do you go for the guy in an off-the-rack rented tux, or for the one in a perfectly cut, perfectly fitting *owned* tuxedo?"

"You can't just—"

"Answer the question, partner."

"Owned," I admitted. "But I'm not falling for a bankrupt guy, either."

James grinned. "I'm not going bankrupt."

"Bold words from a man spending like a drunken sailor."

"I don't need to cash in the 401(k) just yet."

"You have a 401(k)?"

"Why? Is that sexy?"

I batted my eyelashes at him. "Depends on the size. Women like a man who can provide."

"Should I have my tax status tattooed on my forehead?"

"A little too showy, I'd say. You'll have to work it into conversation."

"And that won't be showy?"

I patted the dashboard. "If you show up in this baby wearing your new tux, you won't have to brag about money."

"And you say men are shallow."

"I didn't say you were shallow. I said you were obsessed with looks."

He exited the interstate onto the downtown streets.

"Fair enough. We pretty much are. But your gender seems all about money."

"It's not so much the money."

"Ha."

"It's the power, all the power things—good height, broad shoulders, confident stance, intelligent, good career and, as it turns out, a really nice SUV."

He deepened his tone to übersexy. "That's because it has tall tires and deep treads."

I raised my fingertips to my chest. "Be still my beating heart."

He grinned along with me.

We made our way into downtown and found a spot in an underground parkade. From there, James led the way to Brookswood, a high-end store near the waterfront. I'd never been inside it. I'd sure never planned to shop here.

"I assume they sell tuxes here," I said as we passed through a tall glass doorway into what felt like a rarefied environment.

It was nearly silent. The lighting was muted. The floor was a plush carpet. The displays and stands were placed far apart. It was clear to me that successful people came here to buy very expensive things.

We'd entered into the purse and shoe section.

I didn't see any price tags on the nearby merchandise. It was probably just as well. The prices would likely freak me out. Good thing we were shopping for James and not for me.

"I think they sell most things," he said.

We stopped and took in the lay of the store.

"How did you pick this place?" I asked.

"Fashion bloggers."

"Seriously?" It was hard to picture James browsing fashion blogs.

"They're pretty obsessive about shoes," he said. "And I have to say, I'm not about to wear any of those tight leather pants."

"I think you'd look awesome in tight leather pants," I said with a straight face.

"Bright red," he said with disgust. "Bright red leather, decorated with steel studs. I'd feel like it was Halloween."

"And you were going as a disco vampire?"

James shuddered.

A well-dressed man approached us.

We turned to greet him, and he offhandedly but obviously took in our outfits.

I was wearing black slacks, a green pullover and a pair of comfortable black flats.

James was dressed in a blue-and-white-striped dress shirt over dark gray slacks.

The store clerk didn't seem impressed by us.

"May I help you, sir?" he asked James.

The expression on the man's face said he thought we'd wandered into the wrong store.

"I hope so," James said. "I'd like to look at a tux."

"Bold start," I muttered under my breath.

James gave me a little shove with his arm.

I took it to mean I wasn't being serious enough.

"A tux?" the clerk echoed. He still seemed skeptical.

"A tux," James said with conviction.

"Then, right this way, sir." The man turned to lead us farther into the store.

"This is making me nervous," I said to James in a low tone.

Like the clerk, I couldn't shake the feeling we didn't belong here. At least, I didn't belong here. I shouldn't speak for James.

It was possible that he shopped at stores like this all the time.

I doubted it—based on what I'd seen of his wardrobe. But I didn't know for sure.

"You need to roll with it," James whispered to me.

"It's your credit card," I said back.

"You think you're getting away unscathed?" he asked, amusement coming into his tone.

"I—"

"They have a ladies' section."

I shook my head. "I can't afford a place like this."

"Think of it as an investment."

"An investment in what?" It wasn't like used clothing appreciated over time.

Vintage dresses in some cases, sure. But I'd have to be royalty or a movie star to have a realistic expectation of that happening.

I was neither.

I was very far from being either.

"In your future," James said.

We stepped onto an escalator.

"I don't need *this* much of an image upgrade," I said.

I thought about the balance in my savings account. I had some money, not a ton, but I'd rather spend it on a new car or a vacation. I knew I wouldn't get the same level of enjoyment out of new clothes.

"Go big or go home," James said.

"In that case, I might have to go home."

He frowned at me. "You bailing on me already, Nat?"

I felt bad about that. "I wasn't…" I tried to frame my thoughts. "I didn't mean it literally. I just didn't expect to drain my savings account on day one."

He seemed to think about that.

We stepped off the escalator and found ourselves in the men's clothing section.

"I'll buy you something," he said.

"Oh, no you won't." That wasn't where I'd been going at all.

I was trying to be realistic. I could change styles, but I couldn't drastically change price ranges like this.

"I didn't think about the cost," he said. "Don't get me wrong, I'm not floating in money. But my salary's got to be higher than yours, plus I get bonuses."

"There's no way you're buying me clothes," I said. "We'll find another way. We'll go to an outlet mall or something. If you do it right, you can get bargains on good stuff."

"You have to know what you're doing," James said.

When I didn't say anything back, he kept talking. "Face it, Nat, we don't know what we're doing."

I couldn't disagree with him on that. We each had zero clues about what we were doing. And zero plus zero was still zero.

"One outfit," he said.

I shook my head but he pretended not to see it.

"One outfit," he repeated. "Something we can take on a test-drive to decide if it's worth the investment."

The clerk stopped and turned to face us, looking rather bored. "In this section we have Remaldi. To the left is Dan Goldenberg. And over there is Mende and Saturday Sweet. Do you have a preference for a designer?"

"I wasn't thinking off-the-rack," James said.

He sounded so posh that I felt a burst of pride.

The clerk's expression faltered, and he seemed to re-evaluate the situation.

At least, it seemed to me that he was reevaluating the situation.

If I was him, I'd be reevaluating the situation.

He'd written James off.

That was a mistake.

Okay, this was kind of fun.

"Of course, sir." The man's tone had changed. His shoulders squared, and his expression became more welcoming.

I was right.

I could tell by the amused twinkle in James's eyes that he saw it, too.

"Right this way," the clerk said. "I'll show you to our tailor. I'm Charles, by the way. Is your purchase for a specific event?"

"My firm has a number of formal and charitable events coming up this fall," James said as we fell into step with Charles.

It was my turn to elbow him.

He was getting a little carried away.

He looked down at me. "What?" he mouthed.

I shook my head and gave him a censorious look.

He just grinned.

The lack of price tags was making me nervous.

I was on my fifth, or maybe it was my sixth dress.

They were all pretty. Some of them fit better than others, but nothing I'd tried on so far was butt ugly.

I realized now as I stared into the mirror just how much I normally factored price into my buying decisions.

"Let's see it," James called to me from outside the fitting room.

We were separated by a heavy blue velvet curtain that hung in a semicircle from big wooden rings.

I stood on a soft carpet in a cubicle with a three-way

mirror, a padded chair, and a set of six hooks along the curved wall.

A salesclerk named Naomi had picked out a dozen dresses for me to try.

I hadn't been allowed to pick my own. Oh, no. James insisted we couldn't trust my taste.

He reminded me that I got to pick out his new SUV. It was his turn to choose something for me.

We'd let Charles run wild with the tux.

Once Charles realized James was a serious customer, his enthusiasm level had risen to impressive heights. Along with the tailor, they'd measured every inch of James, consulted me on fabrics and cuts and accessories, until they finally seemed satisfied with the order.

James had remained stoic throughout the process.

I knew he'd spent a fortune. But he'd assured me he could afford it, and he insisted it was my turn next.

I told myself to forget about the prices. For once in my life, I was going to indulge without guilt.

I drew back the curtain.

James stood nearby. Naomi had offered him a chair and a drink, but he'd refused both.

"Well?" I asked, trying to gauge his expression.

"It's better than the last one."

"I liked the last one."

It had been black with a pretty lace bodice, a V-neck and an A-line skirt that draped to midcalf. You could dress it up or dress it down. It would be very versatile.

"That one was too librarian." There was a glint of humor in James's eyes.

"Ha ha," I said, grimacing in his direction.

"This one has more drama," Naomi said.

"You have to match my tux," James said.

"Match your tux?" I asked.

"For the test-drive."

"Your tux is coming with me?"

I don't know what I'd expected in a test-drive. But it wasn't a date with James.

But now I was thinking about a date with James.

I couldn't stop thinking about a date with James—tall, striking, handsome James, with the new shoulder set in his custom-fit tux, and his great new SUV.

The image was sexy.

He was sexy.

I found my gaze stuck on his sexiness.

It was more potent than I'd ever imagined.

How had I missed that?

"And me in the tux," he said, his deep tone only reinforcing my attraction to him.

Uh-oh. I was attracted to James. This was not good.

"Turn," he said to me.

I was happy to do it. It hid my expression. I didn't want him to figure out what I was thinking.

I couldn't be attracted to James.

James was Brooklyn's. Or at least, he used to be Brooklyn's. From the time we were teenagers, he had dated one of my best friends. And now we were buddies, pals, wingpersons for each other.

I didn't dare let attraction into the mix.

"That's nice," he said from behind me. "I like the crisscross, very sexy."

I felt my skin heat in reaction to his words.

He thought I was sexy.

No, no, no, a little voice said inside my head.

He thought the dress was sexy. It was the dress, not me.

It was shimmering green, with a scooped neckline and spaghetti straps that melded into a crisscross pattern over my bare back. It was fitted over my hips, the ankle-length skirt gently flaring out at my thighs. The fabric was light, and I liked the way it moved when I walked.

"Does it come in purple?" James asked.

I turned back to him. "Purple? Really?"

I wouldn't say I was a purple kind of person. I felt exotic enough going with the emerald green. I was already out of my comfort zone.

"A dark plum or maybe boysenberry," he said.

I stared at him in silence for a moment.

"We can have one made through our supplier," Naomi said. "It'll only take a couple of days."

"Boysenberry?" I asked. "That's a very specific color."

"I read," he said. "I learn from all those blogs. And boysenberry will look good with your eyes."

I got a little shiver, maybe a little thrill at the idea that James had been studying my eyes.

I was staring into his right now.

I was staring deeply into his. They were dark deep midnight blue, and they were making me warm all over.

"It'll bring out the highlights in her hair, too," Naomi said.

"I don't have highlights in my hair." All I really did with my hair was grow it.

"But you do," she said. "It's chestnut and gold and copper. You have great hair."

"Really?" I pulled the ends of my hair in front of my eyes.

"You have really great hair," Naomi said. "You should think about doing some layers around your face. Do you put it up?"

"Not really." I didn't think the looped ponytail I used during yoga class would count.

"Don't get rid of the length at the back," Naomi said, scrutinizing me as she talked. "You can do pretty much anything you want with it now. But soften it around your face a bit. It'll look awesome."

I'd never thought much about my hair, my plain brown straight hair. I'd never imagined someone would call it awesome.

"You could stand to lighten it a bit," James said.

I turned my attention back to him. "You don't like my hair."

"I like it a lot," he said. "But I thought you wanted something different."

He was right. I did.

"Go with something semipermanent," Naomi said. "That way you'll keep all the complexity and natural highlights. Just lighten it a shade or two."

"How do you know so much about hair?" I asked her.

"My sister's a hairdresser. Do you have contact lenses?"

I shook my head. I'd tried contacts once, but my eyes couldn't seem to get used to them. It hadn't seemed worth it at the time.

"Too bad," Naomi said. She leaned a little closer to me so James wouldn't hear. "You might want to think about getting some." She canted her head in James's direction. "He likes your eyes."

I opened my mouth to explain the situation, but James jumped in.

"We should probably get your sister's name," he said to Naomi.

Sophie swung open her apartment door and froze.

Her eyes went wide as she stared at me. "What did you *do*?"

"You don't like it?" I was feeling incredibly self-conscious about my new hair and really weird about my contacts.

I got the haircut just this afternoon. Nobody but me and Naomi's sister had seen it so far. I'd been practicing with the contacts for three days now, but I still felt like I was blinking way too often. And I was fighting a constant urge to rub my eyes.

"Are you kidding?" Sophie asked. "I *love* the new you!"

She pulled me into a hug and she whispered in my ear. "Ethan's going to love it, too. Great move, Nat."

"Ethan?" I asked.

I didn't think I'd given Ethan a single thought since the end of our second "date," where he seemed about as interested in me as I was in him.

"Nice to see you again, Nat." It was Bryce's voice.

"Bryce is here?" I asked, pulling from Sophie's hug.

This was supposed to be girls' pizza night at Sophie's apartment.

"Surprise," Sophie said. "I knew it would be more fun with all four of us."

"All four?" Then I spotted Ethan.

He was sitting on one end of Sophie's cream-colored sofa.

Bryce had stood up from the love seat and was looking at me.

"Hi, Bryce," I said. "Hi, Ethan." I smiled to cover my disappointment.

I liked Bryce quite a lot. And Ethan was okay, too. But it was a strain to carry on a conversation with them. And I really wasn't excited about another deep dive into the ongoing adventures of BRT Innovations.

I loved Sophie, I truly did. But hanging out for hours on end with three people who were working on the same all-encompassing project grew tiring.

I wanted to talk to Sophie, just Sophie. I had a lot going on in my life, too.

Not that I would tell her the reasons behind my make-over, or my deal with James, or my weird feelings about James. Still, I wanted girl talk, generic talk about men and relationships, maybe clothes and jewelry. I didn't know.

I did know that 3-D printed desserts wasn't where my head was at tonight.

I dropped my bag on her entry table and headed for the sofa. I would have kicked off my shoes, but everyone else still wore theirs.

I gave an inward sigh as I sat down.

Sophie and I had planned on making mango margaritas tonight, our secret recipe. I supposed that was off, too.

Bryce took his seat again.

"A Hawaiian and a pepperoni?" Sophie asked all three of us.

"Sounds good," Bryce said.

"I prefer vegetarian if nobody minds," Ethan said.

"I'm easy." The last thing I was worried about was the pizza toppings.

Sophie took out her phone. "Don't you love Nat's hair?" she asked as she pulled up the number.

Ethan looked at me, taking in my hair.

I resisted the urge to fluff it or toss my head. The actions seemed appropriate, but too lighthearted for the expression on his face.

"You changed it?" he asked.

"I like it," Bryce said.

"It's lighter," I said to Ethan. "Thanks," I said to Bryce.

"She cut it, too," Sophie said. "Where did you have it done?" Then she got distracted by something on her screen.

Bryce rose and pulled his wallet from his back pocket, extracting a credit card and handing it to Sophie.

I had to admit, it struck me as gentlemanly.

It reminded me of James and how we'd argued but he'd insisted on buying a pair of shoes to go with my dress.

The upshot was that I never did find out the prices. I probably never would.

"I don't know why women insist on doing that to their hair," Ethan said to no one in particular. "Ammonia, peroxide, p-phenylenediamine, diaminobenzene, toluene-2, 5-diamine, resorcinol. It's not exactly a healthy brew."

"Beauty," Sophie said without looking up.

Now I felt like my hair might just blanket the entire Pacific Northwest in a fog of noxious gas.

"If nobody did it," Ethan countered, "if you all went natural, all with the lowest common denominator, then nobody would have to put toxic chemicals on their head."

"I'll tweet that out," Sophie said. "Likely nobody's ever thought about it."

She made me smile.

"Did you hear back from North Capital?" Bryce asked.

"Nothing yet," Ethan said.

"It's after five. I thought the committee was deciding today."

"That was the schedule," Ethan said.

"That's not good," Bryce said.

I was curious, but I wasn't about to ask a naive question about their business, not after my experiences the last couple of times I'd tried.

"It's just one fund," Sophie said. "We shouldn't let it discourage us."

"If we don't get the investment ball rolling soon..." Bryce shook his head.

A light went on inside mine. North Capital was an investment firm. Ethan had said they were looking for investors into BRT Innovations.

There, I had it.

I felt better.

Wait. No. It didn't sound like it was good news.

"Maybe we'll hear tomorrow," Sophie said, obviously trying to be upbeat. "They would have been meeting all afternoon, right? They could have finished after business hours."

"I suppose," Bryce said. He paused. "You're right. Worrying is premature."

I was glad to hear that. I wanted Sophie to be successful. I might not want to hear every single detail of their progress, but I'd sure be her biggest cheerleader if their invention got traction.

"It's the same thing with shoes," Ethan said.

I looked at him in confusion along with everyone else.

He didn't seem to notice. "Do you know the physiological damage done by wearing high heels?"

I had a feeling he was going to explain it to us.

"Dude," Bryce said. "Don't talk them out of high heels."

"You're willing to risk permanent ankle injury so your girlfriend looks sexy?"

Bryce didn't seem to know how to answer that.

"It's okay," Sophie said to Bryce, patting his arm. "We can risk the ankle damage."

I didn't exactly disagree with Ethan. But as a woman who'd only just jumped into the sexy shoe world, I wasn't thrilled with the idea of having them suddenly go out of fashion.

"I'm just saying—" Ethan began.

"That looks don't matter," Sophie said. "Well, I don't believe you. If looks didn't matter to men, women wouldn't go to all the trouble."

"You dress for each other," Ethan said.

"That's not true," I said.

I had it on good authority, James's authority, that men liked glamorous women.

"Studies have confirmed it," Ethan said.

"You'll have to show me those studies," Sophie said. "Pizza will be here in twenty minutes."

I was glad of that, too.

I was hungry, and I was hoping we'd break out some kind of alcoholic beverage.

Ethan turned his attention to his phone.

"Are we making margaritas?" I asked Sophie.

She looked regretful. "Do you mind beer? Bryce brought some imported beer."

"Sure," I said.

Beer didn't strike me as strong enough, since I was pretty certain Ethan was looking up the studies that showed women dressed for each other.

I wasn't going through all this to impress other women.

I wanted to impress men, men like James.

I wanted to impress James.

Oh, man. This was getting bad.

I really needed that margarita.

Five

I felt like a movie star.

The feeling lasted for about thirty seconds. And then I felt like an impostor.

I'd never had my hair professionally styled before. I mean, sure, I'd had it cut plenty of times. But I'd never gone to a hairstylist to get it put up for a special event—not even the day I was supposed to be Brooklyn's bridesmaid.

I'd found myself liking Naomi's sister Madeline. She was upbeat and positive, and she pushed me just enough to be adventurous without completely freaking me out.

I'd gone back to her a second time, and she'd done an amazing job on my hair. It was soft around my face and gathered in a loose braid that somehow swirled into a messy bun at the back of my head. The new highlights really showed up under my bathroom lights and seemed to give it added texture.

Madeline had talked me into a mani-pedi—a new experience for me.

I'd thought about pedicures on a few spa days. But

I preferred a good deep-tissue massage to almost anything else. I once had a facial, but I wasn't wild about them.

Now my finger- and toenails were perfectly shaped, perfectly even, and shimmering with a subtle purple Madeline had called oyster mauve. I was almost afraid to use my hands.

I didn't have a lot of jewelry to choose from, and the outfit seemed to need something more dramatic than my usual studs or hoops. I searched the bottom of my jewelry box and found a set of long dangling crystal chain earrings with a matching necklace. They worked, and I was set.

Thank goodness.

I only had five minutes to spare.

I carefully strapped on the exotic shoes James had bought for me. I'd never owned four-inch heels before. They were sharp black on the soles, silver on the inner heel, with silver straps dotted with white and purple crystals.

They were wild.

I stood up in them and practiced my new walking style. For a few seconds, I felt wild.

Then I was back to impostor again.

I took one last glimpse in my full-length mirror, telling myself I could do this. I could go out in public and nobody would guess this wasn't really me.

My stomach started jumping in protest, but there was a knock on my door, and I had no choice but to go.

I opened the door to James.

His eyes widened a bit and he sucked in a breath. It was hard to tell what that meant.

First I wondered if he was reacting to me. And then I wondered if he was actually looking past me into my apartment. He'd never been here before. And Sophie told me all the time that "early industrial" was not going to impress people.

Brooklyn's place had always been tasteful, up-to-date and immaculate. It stood to reason that James would prefer elegance to utilitarianism.

"Hi," I finally said to break the awkward silence.

"You…"

I glanced over my shoulder. "I know it's a bit unusual. But it's quite functional."

"Huh?" he asked.

"My place," I said, gesturing. "I know it's ugly."

He looked over my shoulder for a beat. Then he looked directly at me.

"You did it," he said.

"Did what?"

He gestured up and down. "That is *some* transformation."

Oh, we weren't talking about my apartment. That was probably good.

"Where are your glasses?" He moved closer. "You got contacts?" He broke into a smile. "That a girl. I'm impressed."

"They feel weird in my eyes." I would admit it wasn't as bad today as the first few days.

"Well, they look great."

"Thanks. You look good, too." I shook myself out of my self-absorption.

He looked fantastic.

His hair was different, too.

I took it in, did a walk-around, and came back to face him.

"The hair looks good." It was shorter on the sides, looking updated instead of classic.

And he'd let the stubble grow out on his chin, giving him a more rakish look, a dangerous look. I found myself wanting to reach out and stroke his face to see what it felt like.

I resisted the urge.

He held out his arms. "The haircut cost a lot less than the tux."

"The tux is off the charts."

His shirt was crisp white. His tie was straight, black with subtle inlaid gray diamonds. We'd gone with my choice on the suit fabric, onyx rather than jet-black. The style looked even better on James than it had on the model in the picture.

James had a perfect physique, tall with broad shoulders, a deep chest and what looked certain to be washboard abs.

I felt a rush of attraction. It felt unnervingly like arousal. I feared my face might be getting flushed with it.

"So, worth the money?" he asked, gesturing to the tux.

"I don't know what you paid, but I see a long lineup of eligible ladies in your future." I didn't like the picture, but I was more than sure it would be true.

He grinned. "Let's hope so. Do you need to get a coat?"

I shook my head. "I don't have anything that'll go with this dress. I'll have to hope the ballroom is heated."

"There'll be five hundred people there. I think you can count on it being warm. And I'll tell the driver to turn up the heat."

"You're not driving your new baby tonight?"

"The theme tonight is Mardi Gras. I see some drinks in my future."

"I could get into a hurricane," I said.

I was definitely partial to fruit juices, rum and blended ice.

I stepped into the hall and locked the door behind him.

"Love the shoes," James said.

"You better."

He'd given me some say in the shoes, but he'd definitely been the one to push for higher heels and the sparkle look.

"I have very good taste." He gazed down for a moment. "And you have even better feet."

"I had professional help," I said. "With the hair, too."

"It all looks good, very chic, very swanky. I predict a lineup of men wanting to dance with you."

We started for the staircase.

"I just hope I don't fall off the shoes," I said.

"A gentleman would hold you up." As he spoke, we came to the top of the staircase.

He offered me his arm.

I took it.

I had no desire to ruin the evening by falling down a flight of stairs.

His arm was strong and warm and reassuring. It felt like I was steadying myself against an immovable plank of wood.

I slid my opposite hand along the railing and felt completely secure all the way down.

We started across the foyer, but he stopped in the middle.

"Do you mind?" he asked.

"Mind what?"

"Just standing there for a minute."

I wondered for a second if he'd brought me a corsage. Then I wondered if it would ruin the line of my dress. Then I told myself I was being ungrateful.

If James had gone to the trouble to bring me a corsage, I was going to smile and thank him, then pin it on my dress no matter what color it might be.

He stepped away from me.

I wondered where he might have hidden the florist box. But to my surprise, he walked around me in a circle, looking, watching, making me feel incredibly self-conscious.

"Well?" I asked as he completed the circle. I felt stupidly nervous and impatient.

"I hate to say it."

"Just spit it out."

If the outfit wasn't working, there was nothing I could do about it now. It wasn't like I had a closet of clothes back upstairs that I could wear to the ball. Like Cinderella, I only had one gown.

"We might be finished."

"For the night?" Maybe I didn't look perfect, but I thought I looked pretty good. I wasn't wild about undoing it all before anybody else even saw the effort.

"Finished making you over." He came closer. His voice went sexy low. "You're absolutely perfect."

I opened my mouth to say I didn't want the evening to be over this soon, but then his words penetrated.

"Wait, what?"

"You," he repeated. "Are perfect. Even your walk. The law of large numbers is going to be massively in your favor tonight. You'll probably fall in love."

I coughed out a laugh. "That's *really* not what I thought you were going to say."

"Well, that's what's true."

"It's a huge exaggeration. But it's nice of you to say so."

"We'll see," he said.

He offered me his arm again.

I took it.

I didn't need it anymore. But I liked holding on to him. I liked the feeling of connection.

He was my partner in crime, after all. He shared my secret, and he was helping me make my life better. It stood to reason those things would make me feel close to him.

* * *

"Wow," I said.

"You do go well with the room," James said.

"I'm afraid I might disappear."

Perimeter lights in the hotel ballroom glowed purple. Icicles of glass crystal hung in streamers from the ceiling. The cloths on stand-up tables were mauve, while tall, bulbous arrangements of white roses picked up the surrounding colors.

A quintet played on a low stage at one end, jazzy piano music wafting over the voices in the big room. Hundreds of people were already there, mixing and mingling, looking impressive in their formal clothes.

"Do you do this a lot?" I asked.

I would have stopped and stared, probably with my mouth hanging open.

But James kept walking. "Me?"

"Yes, you. Does your firm send you to parties like this all the time?"

"Never," he said.

My steps faltered for a moment. "Are we crashing?"

James stopped. "What? *No.* I bought tickets. But I don't usually like this kind of thing."

"I never do this kind of thing."

"Buck up, Nat. It's good as a test-drive."

I silently reminded myself why we were here and what we were doing.

I'd started feeling like this was a date.

It wasn't a date. I was James's wing-person, and he was mine.

I glanced around as we walked and noticed how many women were surreptitiously checking him out.

"Do you see that?" he asked.

"I sure do."

"They're impressed."

"They are definitely impressed." More and more women turned to watch him.

I leaned in closer to his ear. "It's the tux."

"The tux?"

"Yes." I knew it was more than just the tux. It was absolutely the man inside the tux. But I wanted James to know he was getting his money's worth on the purchase.

"They're not looking at me," he said.

"They're absolutely looking at you—all of you, the whole package of you."

"The *men*?"

"What men?"

"The men who are staring at you."

"Nobody's staring at me. I'm talking about the women. There are a dozen women looking at you right now."

"Well, there are two dozen men looking at you. One of them just pointed."

I threw James a subtle elbow. "Ha ha."

"I wasn't joking."

I moved my attention from the women to the men in the area.

It was true. A few of them were looking my way.

I didn't buy the pointing thing, but it was gratifying to know my dress was working.

"You're getting your money's worth out of the dress, too," I said.

"I'm not getting my money's worth. It's them who are getting my money's worth. Which, when I think about it, isn't really fair, it is?"

I could hear the smile in his voice.

"You want to stand back and point at me?" I asked in an equally teasing tone.

"I think I should abandon you."

I didn't know how to take that. "What? Are you annoyed about something?"

"So they can approach you, Nat. None of them are going to ask you to dance with me standing here."

I could see his point. But I wasn't exactly ready to be left alone here.

"Maybe in a few minutes," I said.

"You can do it."

"No. I can't. I really don't think I—"

He was walking away.

"James." I didn't want to shout.

No, scratch that. I did want to shout. I wanted to shout at him to get back here and help me. This wasn't our deal. My wingman wasn't supposed to fly off in the first thirty seconds.

But he was gone, swallowed by the crowd of people.

I stood still for a few minutes, wondering how not to look like an interloper.

Conversational groups surrounded me, two and three, some groups of up to six people. They seemed to know each other. They were chatting and laughing.

I wanted to sprint for the exit.

I thought about taking temporary refuge in the ladies' room. But then I ordered myself to buck up. I couldn't hide and meet men at the same time.

The law of large numbers. That's why I was here.

I caught sight of a bar lineup and decided it was a halfway measure. Lining up for a drink wasn't the same as hiding, and it would give me something to do other than standing here looking pathetically lonely.

I joined the longest line, hoping it would take a while.

The man in front of me turned.

He was about five-ten, dark blond hair, a very nice suit and a friendly face.

I smiled at him. "Hello."

He nodded. "Hi. Are you from the hospital?"

I wondered if I looked like a nurse. "The hospital?"

"St. Michaels…the recipient of tonight's fundraising."

"Oh."

Well, didn't I feel stupid. It hadn't occurred to me to ask James about the event. I was too focused on my dress and shoes.

"My date is with O'Neil Nybecker," I said.

Then I realized I'd just told him I had a date. Perfect. I was really starting off with a bang here.

"You haven't made it very far," a woman said to him, arriving to link arms with him.

"You were fast, sweetheart," he said to her.

He turned to me. "This is…"

"I'm Nat Remington. I was just saying my date is with O'Neil Nybecker."

Since he wasn't single, I was definitely glad to have claim to a date. I didn't want this man's date to get the wrong idea about me. I wasn't poaching.

"Nice to meet you," the woman said with a friendly smile. "Harold is on the St. Michaels board."

The man held his hand out to me. "Harold Schmidt."

I shook his hand. "Hello, Harold."

The line moved.

"Here we go," I said.

"Ah, yes. This is better," he said.

They both turned to move a few steps.

A man in line directly behind me spoke up. "Did I hear you say O'Neil Nybecker?"

I turned to look at him.

He was younger, maybe in his early twenties. He was clean-shaven, tall and fit. His hair was close cropped on the sides, shaved almost bald, while it was long at the top, thick and fluffed up.

He looked cocky and confident.

"I did," I answered.

The line moved again, and I moved with it.

"I'm from O'Neil Nybecker. Just started a couple of weeks ago. Do you work there, too?"

"I don't. I work in the public library."

He gave a winning smile. "So you came with someone from the firm. Do I dare hope you're here with a friend and not a lover?"

I wanted to tell him it was none of his business. The question was almost rudely blunt.

Then I told myself to chill. It might have been awkwardly phrased, but he was only trying to decide if I was attached. Probably so he didn't make the same mistake I'd just made and have my date show up all of a sudden.

Not that I'd been flirting with the guy in front of me. I was only making chitchat. Still, his "sweetheart" showing up like that had taken me by surprise.

"A friend," I said.

The man held out his hand to shake. "Aaron Simms. I'm an economist."

I shook. "Nat Remington."

"Nat is short for Natalie?"

"Natasha."

"Ohhhh." He made a point of looking impressed. "A beautiful name for a beautiful woman."

"Are you here with a date?" I asked in return.

If he was with a date, he probably shouldn't be flirting with me.

"I'm here on my own. It's a corporate thing. I want to impress the brass."

"The brass cares about this kind of thing, do they?"

I couldn't help remembering that James said he never went to functions like this.

Aaron leaned in and lowered his voice. "I'm showing enthusiasm for the firm. You want to get ahead, you play all the angles."

"And this is an angle?" I had to admit, I was intrigued.

I'd never been one for office politics. Not that there were many politics in the public library. Then again, the last promotion I'd been in line for had unexpectedly gone to someone else. She was very socially astute, organizing outings and events for the staff.

Maybe I should pay more attention.

The line moved again, and I kept pace.

"I'm young, eager, a good conversationalist and dancer. I know which fork to use, and I know how to get the O'Neil Nybecker name out there. Why do you think they donate to the hospital?"

It seemed like a trick question. "To help sick people get well?"

Aaron chuckled as if I was delightfully naive. "Corporate reputation, darlin'."

Darlin'? Seriously, *darlin'*?

He kept talking. "They throw their money at prominent causes, especially those near and dear to the mayor's heart. It makes them look like they care, softens the edges of their hard-nosed corporate focus. Did you see the mayor? He's here with his wife. She's a big supporter of the arts center. Guess which cause O'Neil Nybecker's supporting next?"

Okay, I could get this one. "The arts center?" I asked, half-sarcastically.

"Now you're catching on."

I grimaced.

Luckily, the Schmidt couple were the only ones left in line in front of me. I'd be out of here soon.

"What are you drinking?" Aaron asked.

I truly did not want him to order my drink.

"I haven't decided yet."

"They do a great Sazerac."

"Oh." I wasn't sure what to say back.

I wasn't about to agree to his recommendation. I was having a hurricane. But I didn't want to disclose that, either. I could be wrong, but I was guessing his plan was to order our drinks together and use it as an excuse to walk away with me.

I didn't want my hair, dress and shoes to work on this guy. No thanks.

"*There* you are." James arrived and looped his arm around my waist.

I gave him a surprised look.

My first impression of Aaron might not have been great, but James couldn't know that.

It surprised me that he was breaking up the conversation.

"Hi, James," I said, framing a what-are-you-doing? question with my expression.

"Simms." James nodded to Aaron.

They knew each other. I guess that should have occurred to me. O'Neil Nybecker was a very big firm with a twenty-story office building, but I supposed there were meetings and a lunch room. People would pass each other in the halls.

"Hi, James." Aaron took in James's arm at my waist. Then he looked back at me. "Friends?" he asked, looking a little bit annoyed.

"Good friends," James said.

The Schmidts took their drinks and moved on.

"What would you like?" James asked me.

"A hurricane, please," I said.

"Coming up," James said.

"Was it what you hoped for?" I asked James as we made our way through the hotel lobby at the end of the evening.

"It was about what I expected." He didn't sound thrilled. "You?"

"It was fun walking in."

After James had rescued me from Aaron, I'd mixed and mingled some more. I'd even danced a few times. But I hadn't met anyone interesting. The law of large numbers seemed to have let me down tonight.

James smiled as we approached the front door of the hotel. "You caused a bit of a ripple with your entrance."

I agreed that I'd attracted a bit of attention. But James was the one who had women craning their necks.

"You caused a bigger ripple. Did those women approach you?"

"A few did. They seemed nice."

"But nothing to write home about?" I asked.

He pushed open the door for me. "Definitely nothing to write home about."

"Do you think we were doing something wrong? Or maybe my expectations were too high. I mean, we definitely look good and all."

"We look great," he said.

"Yeah, I think we do." I couldn't imagine any woman not falling all over James the way he looked tonight, that was for sure.

I'd fall all over him myself if I thought there was any chance he'd reciprocate. And that wasn't just the two hurricanes talking. He was hot.

"We'll have to try again," he said.

He looked both ways on the hotel driveway and signaled for our car.

"Try the same thing?" I asked.

"There'll be different people at a different event. I don't think we should abandon this approach just yet. O'Neil Nybecker is a sponsor of the arts-center fund-raiser coming up."

"Aaron mentioned that," I said.

James's brow went up. "Oh?"

"Uh-huh," I said.

There was a bit of an edge to James's voice. "What else did he say?"

"Is there something you don't like about Aaron?"

"There are a few things I don't like about Aaron. What did he say to you?"

I realized Aaron wasn't the most appealing person in the world. "He said he attended events like this to impress the brass."

James gave a cool laugh as the car pulled up in front of us. "That sounds like Aaron."

"He seemed harmless enough," I said. "A bit annoying maybe. A bit young."

James opened the back door. "A bit nakedly ambitious."

"Is ambitious bad?" I asked as I climbed into the car.

Aaron had been clear about wanting to climb the corporate ladder. But lots of people wanted to get ahead.

"Depends on how you do it." James closed my door and went around to the other side.

"How is Aaron doing it?" I asked while James got settled.

I remembered I was thinking about my own lost promotion while Aaron had been talking about his approach to his career development.

"Well, he's got a big leg up, that's for sure."

"Because he's smart? Hardworking? Ambitious?"

The car pulled smoothly away from the curb.

"Because he's a Simms."

"That's a good thing?" I guessed.

"His uncle is Horatio Simms, senior partner at O'Neil Nybecker. Word on the street is that it may soon become O'Neil Nybecker Simms."

"Ahhh," I said. *Ahhh* was how I felt hearing that information.

"Aaron is entitled and cavalier," James said with a frown. "And last week he became my special problem."

That piqued my curiosity. "Why? What did he do?"

"I've been asked to show him the ropes. He's an intern."

"He didn't tell me he was an intern."

Aaron hadn't sounded at all like he was in a training position.

"I'm not surprised," James said. "But let's stop talking about Aaron. I'll worry about him Monday morning."

"One last question?" I asked.

James frowned. "About Aaron?"

"Let's call it Aaron adjacent."

"All right. I'll give you one more. But only since you look so gorgeous."

I tried not to smile, but I couldn't help it. His teasing compliment made me feel good.

I should stop letting James make me feel good. I should at least try to stop it.

"He said the brass is impressed if you attend functions like this. But you said you never attend them. I wondered why not."

There was an edge to James's voice when he spoke. "Maybe I don't care about impressing the brass."

It was clear I'd asked the wrong question. But we'd pledged to be honest with each other. And I had to wonder if James's instincts might not be leading him astray on this one. Women were definitely attracted to money and power, and moving up in a firm like O'Neil Nybecker would only increase James's power and therefore his desirability to large numbers of women.

We were going after large numbers here.

"What would it hurt?" I pressed. "You went tonight. I mean, I know it wasn't the success we'd hoped for, but it wasn't exactly painful, either. Your bosses saw you there. If they liked it—"

"I'm an economist, not a show pony." His sharp response took me by surprise. "There are people who get ahead by playing games, and those who get ahead through solid, hard work. Maybe I don't want to compromise."

His reaction threw me.

"I thought that was the point of all this? I thought we were playing the image game. All we're doing here is compromising."

"In our personal lives," he said. "Not in our professional lives."

"I was thinking it might work for both. And maybe it only works if we do both. Maybe we need to change all the way through, not just on the surface, not just on the weekends or when we're together playing dress up."

"You want us to compromise all the way through?"

"I'm not saying we compromise our ethics or anything." I wasn't sure where I was going with this, but so far, it sounded okay. "I'm saying where's the harm in being more exciting on all levels? Look at me."

He did.

I gestured to the outfit. "I'm all dressed up. But I'm still librarian Nat Remington. I have her opinions. I have her hobbies. I have her attitude. I have her plain old name. Aaron said Natasha was a pretty name."

"Aaron again?"

"Stop. Seriously. Don't let Aaron mess with your mood. Natasha is a pretty name. But I went with Nat. Why did I go with Nat? Tasha is the better nickname. It's gorgeous. It's exotic. It's the name of someone who leads a wild and glamorous life."

"So change it," James said.

"I might."

"You should."

"I will." I felt empowered just making the pledge.

"Good."

"You change yours, too."

He gave me a look of skepticism. "How can you change James?"

"Jamie. You can be Jamie."

"I don't—"

I reached out and touched his arm. "You promised to trust my judgment. You need a new name, something less uptight than James."

"Seriously?"

"Yes."

"Okay."

"Really?" I couldn't help but feel excited.

"Yes, really. So, tell me, what are Jamie and Tasha going to do next?"

Six

We decided on a popular dance club.

James picked out my dress again, but this time I paid for it.

I kind of loved it. It was a shimmery gold-and-black geometric pattern, sleeveless, with a scoop neck. Tight to the waist, it had a gold metal belt over a pleated skirt. The soft skirt hung to my midthigh and swirled when I danced.

The following Friday, I left my hair down and found some dangling gold earrings that looked flashy enough for the occasion.

James argued for gold sandals, but we settled on black cutout ankle boots with tapered heels. They were easier to wear, but still had a funky, avant-garde appeal. I never would have considered them before now.

We stood in line for half an hour. The club was loud and crowded, with lots of techno music, flashing laser lights and haze from a fog machine behind the DJ.

It wasn't to my taste, but I danced a lot. I couldn't talk to any of my partners, so I had no idea if I liked them or not. Mostly, they grinned at me while we danced, then they bid me a silent adieu with a wave of their hand before moving on to another partner.

Finally, James touched my arm and pointed to the exit.

My ears were throbbing, the music following us outside as we found our way into the fresh air. It was misty, and a skiff of wet from some earlier rain made the black pavement shine under the lights.

He asked me a question, but I couldn't hear.

"What?" I asked in what I hoped was a loud voice. I couldn't hear myself very well, either.

He leaned into my ear. "What did you think?"

I gave him a shrug while we passed the lineup of more people crowding the sidewalk, waiting to go inside.

Some of the outfits made mine look tame.

"Not my thing," he said.

"Mine, either," I admitted, although it had been my suggestion.

We made our way down the block to the brighter lights of First Avenue.

"Let's scratch it off the list," he said.

"Consider it scratched."

My feet hurt, but I liked walking.

"Hungry?" he asked.

"Starving." I was.

He pointed to a brick café with big awnings and glowing lights. "Try that?"

"Yes, please."

The sooner I sat down, the happier I'd be.

A hostess showed us to a booth beside the window. It looked out on a patio that was empty now since rain was beginning to sprinkle down again.

"This is nice," I said, settling into the cushy seat and opening a big menu on the table in front of me.

James did the same. "So, did Tasha meet anyone?"

I grinned as I read my way through the burger selection, thinking a chocolate milkshake sounded awesome. "Tasha met a whole bunch of people."

"Did she like any of them?"

I glanced up to see his gaze on me.

"She couldn't tell. I didn't have a single conversation. What about Jamie? Anyone interesting for you?"

He shook his head. "Same thing. Lots of inanely grinning maniac dancers."

"Is Jamie being judgmental?"

"Jamie is being realistic. Dance clubs are *so* scratched off our list."

"I do like the outfit," I said, making a point of taking in his distressed jeans, white-and-gold foil-patterned T-shirt and short leather jacket.

"Never going to wear this shirt again," he said. "What are you having?"

"Maybe you could do yard work or paint in it or something."

"You're too practical for your own good."

"If you don't want it, I'll take it."

"You think it's girlie?"

"I didn't say that."

"It'll be way too big for you."

"I can sleep in it." As the words left my mouth, our gazes met.

They meshed and melded and the air seemed to sizzle between us.

I didn't think I was imagining it.

"What can I get for you?" a waitress asked, stopping beside the table.

James broke the look.

He moved his attention to the menu. "I'll take a bacon mushroom burger with fries."

"Anything to drink?"

"Cola," he said.

I willed my heart rate to slow down.

I wished my skin didn't prickle. I knew I had goose bumps, and I knew exactly why. There was no point in even pretending I didn't have a crush on James... Jamie. It was Jamie now, and he was hot.

"And for you?" the waitress asked.

"Cheeseburger," I said. "With fries and a chocolate shake." I definitely needed the shake to cool me down. And drowning my arousal in delicious calories seemed like a really great idea right now.

"A shake sounds good," Jamie said. "Can I switch?"

"Certainly," the woman said. "Coming right up."

"Thanks," Jamie said, handing her his menu.

I did the same.

"We have to come up with something else," I said before we could take the conversation back to me sleeping in his shirt. Even though I was staring at the shirt, thinking of how it would feel skimming over my skin and how Jamie would look without it.

Whoa.

"Something else?" he asked.

"Another exciting activity for Jamie and Tasha." I forced a light note into my voice. "Exactly how brave are we? Are we going bungee jumping or skydiving?"

"Is that what you want to do?" He looked serious.

I'd been joking.

"Nah," I said, thinking it through. "It would be over so fast, and we wouldn't meet anyone on the way down."

He didn't answer, and his gaze focused outside the window.

The rain was increasing, bouncing off the tables and

chairs on the patio and streaking through the bands from the streetlights.

Jamie frowned, and I wondered if he was worried about flagging a cab.

"Don't worry," I said.

He looked back at me. "About jumping out of a plane? I'll jump out of a plane if that's what you want."

"I thought you were worried about getting a cab."

He looked confused. "Why would I worry about that?"

"The rain," I offered.

"It's Seattle," he said. "The system can handle rain."

"Then why are you frowning?"

"I'm not frowning."

"You were. You frowned when you looked out the window just now."

"Oh, that frown."

"Did I say something wrong?" I went over the past couple of minutes inside my head, trying to figure out what it could have been.

"It wasn't you. I thought I saw someone out there."

I was relieved, but only a little bit. I didn't want Jamie to feel upset about something I said or about anyone else.

"Who was it?" I asked, hoping to make it better.

"It doesn't matter. It wasn't them."

I knew I shouldn't press, but I couldn't help but be curious. "You can talk to me. Remember, we're going to be honest with each other. You said it was the only way this was going to work."

"Fine," he said. "Sure. Why not."

I braced myself, not sure what to expect.

"I thought I saw Aaron."

Okay, that wasn't at all what I'd expected. "From your office Aaron?"

"That Aaron."

I'd met Aaron a second time on a night Jamie and I went shopping. It was clear he and Jamie didn't get along particularly well. But I didn't understand why merely seeing Aaron would annoy Jamie.

"We're not that far from O'Neil Nybecker," I said. "Maybe he was working late."

"I *wish* he was working late. He cut out early today… again."

I still wasn't seeing why Jamie cared. I tried to make a joke. "I take it you don't have flexible hours?"

"Not for interns. And not after the stunt he pulled this week."

Again, I was curious, but I didn't know if the incident would be confidential.

I waited, but Jamie didn't elaborate.

The waitress dropped off our milkshakes.

He was still frowning, and he didn't take a drink.

I sipped through the straw, and the milkshake was delicious.

"Do you want to talk about it?" I asked.

"I don't want to bore you."

"Go ahead. I'll tell you if I get bored."

Jamie tried his own milkshake.

"Good, huh?" I prompted.

"It is."

"So?" I wanted to know what had the power to make him frown like that.

"It sounds minor, but it's not. In a meeting with one of our biggest clients, where, as an intern, he's supposed to sit quietly and learn, Aaron pops up with a *suggestion*."

Jamie paused, and I waited.

I stirred my milkshake with the straw, pretending I wasn't dying of curiosity.

"He says," Jamie finally continued, "and I quote, 'Take

the company public.'" Jamie's expression told me he was disgusted.

"And that's a bad idea?" I was guessing, of course. I didn't know anything about it.

"It's a risky idea," Jamie said. "Worse, it's a knee-jerk idea. It's a gut reaction. We don't do gut reactions. We do thoughtful and thorough analysis. Even if it was the best idea in the world, even if we'd done the research, you don't blurt it out in front of the client without a plan. The team had no plan."

"Would you ever go with your gut?" I asked. "Make a risky decision based on your instincts?"

"Never."

I'd never do that, either. At least Nat would never do that. I wasn't sure about Tasha. Tasha just might.

"What about Jamie?" I asked.

Jamie looked confused.

"I get that James is careful, but would Jamie take a flier on something?"

Jamie's eyes narrowed and the corners of his mouth went white. "Are you suggesting Jamie should be more like Aaron?"

I tried to figure out how to call the question back.

But the waitress appeared with two laden plates.

"One cheeseburger," she said, putting a plate down in front of me. "One bacon mushroom." She set Jamie's plate down. "Will there be anything else?"

I shook my head to answer her. I wasn't hungry anymore. I was feeling a little sick.

"We're good," Jamie said to her. "Thanks."

She walked away.

"I didn't mean that," I said.

"Jamie's not careless," he said.

"I'm sorry."

"Don't worry about it. Let's just eat."

But I was worried about it.

I took a bite of my burger and forced myself to eat some fries. But my heart wasn't in it.

Jamie might not be careless. But I was beginning to worry Tasha was.

I didn't hear from Jamie all week.

Sophie called to see if I would meet up Friday night. But I was afraid she'd bring Bryce and Ethan along, so I lied and said I had plans with the girls from work.

By Thursday, I couldn't bring myself to look at my new clothes. After work, I stuffed them to the back of my closet and changed into my oldest and most Nat-like outfit, deciding to garden until I was ready to go to sleep.

I pulled back my hair and tied it up in a scarf. Then I propped open the patio doors to let in the fresh air and tucked my hands into my floral-print garden gloves.

There was a knock on my door.

I ignored it at first, thinking it was probably Sophie. She might be frustrated that I'd turned down her invitation and decided to bring Bryce and Ethan directly to me.

Wouldn't she be surprised to have me greet them all like this? Ha. Ethan would be well and truly cured of any lingering desire to date me then.

The knock sounded again, this time more forcefully.

Fine.

If she wanted to surprise me, I would surprise her right back. For better or worse, this was Natasha Remington. I wear old clothes. I garden. I'm plain and boring, and I like it that way.

It would have been perfect if I already had a cat.

I went for the door, wrenching it open.

It was Jamie.

"Hey, Tasha." He breezed past me. "I have an idea."

I stood with the door wide-open, staring at him.

He glanced around at the decor but didn't react. He turned back to me. He didn't react to my outfit, either.

"I don't understand," I said.

"That's because I haven't told you yet."

"Told me what?"

"My idea. Didn't I just say I had an idea? That's why I'm here."

"But…"

"Rock climbing," he said.

I didn't have a response.

"Wait." He seemed to notice what I was wearing. "Are you…renovating?"

That I could answer. "Gardening. What do you mean rock climbing?"

"Want some help?"

I took in his slacks and dress shirt. "You don't look dressed to get dirty."

He glanced down at himself. "I suppose."

I closed the door behind me. "What are you saying about rock climbing?"

"You and me. Instead of jumping out of a plane, we take some training and go climbing. It'll be exciting and adventurous. And it'll get us out to meet regular people, not the club or ballroom set."

"Have you ever done it before?" I asked.

"Never. You?"

I shook my head.

"I saw a beginners class advertised. It starts on Saturday over near Ballard. We could sign up."

I took my gloves off. "Did I miss something?"

"Miss what?"

"I thought you were ticked off at me."

He looked puzzled. "Why?"

I really didn't want to bring it up again. "The argument…last weekend…at the café."

"I told you not to worry about that."

"You didn't sound sincere."

"Well, I was. Are you that thin-skinned?"

I felt my back go up. "Excuse me?"

"Do you want me to apologize for disagreeing with you?"

"No." I tossed the gloves down. "And I'm not thin-skinned. But you were clearly annoyed with me, and then you didn't call."

"Should I have called?"

"You're missing my point."

He moved a little closer. "I'm sorry. What's your point?"

"You got mad, and then you went silent, and I didn't know what to think."

"You're forgetting the 'don't worry about it' that came in between those two things."

"You can't just toss something off like that and expect it to land. I thought our project was over. I thought you were giving up."

"Are *you* giving up?"

"No." Well, I was. At least, I had been. But I didn't want to.

He gently took my hands. "I'm not giving up."

I felt his touch all the way up my arms and into my chest.

I had an overpowering urge to lean forward, to press my chest against his and to wrap my arms around him. I wanted to hug him. I wanted to kiss him. I wanted to… Oh, boy.

I swallowed.

"So, what do you say?" he asked.

Yes! I almost shouted.

"Shall we learn how to rock climb?" he asked.

"Yes," I said out loud. "Let's learn how to rock climb."

He hugged me.

He pulled me against his chest and wrapped his strong arms around me and hugged me to him.

My body sighed. It sang. I hugged him back, leaned my cheek against his chest, closed my eyes and absorbed the heat and the energy pulsing from him into me.

Time seemed to stop.

I felt his breath on my hair.

His chest expanded with a deep breath. Then his arms pulled more tightly around me.

I pretended it was attraction.

I let myself fantasize that he liked the feel of me, the scent of me, that he wanted to taste my lips the way I was dying to taste his.

Too soon, he drew back.

He turned away and cleared his throat.

I was mortified to think he could tell how I felt.

Had I hugged him too tight? The way my body had gone boneless and molded to his had to be a dead give-away. He was embarrassed. He probably pitied me.

I pitied myself.

I had to get over this infatuation.

"Is there a website or something?" I asked, trying desperately to sound normal. "Where we sign up?"

His shoulders were tense, and he didn't turn. "I'll take care of it."

"I don't mind—"

"I'll take care of it."

"Okay." I waited for him to look at me, but he didn't.

"Uh, Jamie?"

"Yes."

I *so* didn't want to have this conversation, but I wouldn't be able to stand another two days of guessing his mood. I'd just done that, and it was awful.

"Is everything okay?" I asked, bracing myself.

"You bet." He turned then, and he smiled. He looked almost normal. "I'm glad you're willing to give it a try."

I was willing to give a whole lot of things a try right now.

But I couldn't tell him that.

Instead, I fought the lingering hum of attraction. I wished mind over matter worked better than it did. But it didn't. Despite logic, reason and my honest-to-goodness best efforts, I couldn't shake the desire to hurl myself into his arms.

"I'm glad you thought of it," I managed to say.

"The class starts at nine on Saturday. Can I pick you up at eight?"

"Yes. Sure. I'll be ready. Is there anything I need to bring?"

"There's a list of suggested attire on the website. I'll send you the link."

"Good. That sounds good." I felt like we were making small talk.

"See you Saturday." He headed for the door.

I stepped out of the way.

When the door closed behind him, I blew out a breath.

I knew I had to get gardening. I had to do something normal. But my feet didn't want to move.

My phone pinged with a text.

It was Jamie, and my heart lurched ridiculously at the sight of his name.

He was sending the link to the climbing website.

I felt like a foolish teenager mooning over that cute boy in math class.

I was way too old for this.

* * *

I took a vacation day on Friday.

I didn't really need the day off, and Nat would never take a sudden, random day off work on a lark. But it felt like something Tasha would do. So I did it. And I was glad.

I was a little restless, but I was still glad.

I sat staring at my gray cinder block walls. I'd lived here three years now, and they were the same color as when I'd first moved in. I'd hung two pictures on them, both in the spots where a previous tenant had drilled a hook.

They were watercolor portraits of four young girls— in one they were smiling, in the other they were thought-ful. Sophie had bought them for me as a housewarming present. She said they reminded her of the four of us: Layla, Brooklyn, her and me.

It was obvious that Brooklyn was the pretty, pink-cheeked blonde. Layla was the intent girl with auburn hair. I was the short brunette with glasses, always the glasses. That was me, always shorter, always a little mousier than the rest.

Sophie had been right. The paintings did look like a peaceful, rather angelic version of the four of us.

I wondered for a minute if actual photos might be even better. I thought I'd like to look at the real us instead of the paintings.

Maybe that was what I would do.

Something Jamie had said was ticking through my mind today.

It had been innocent enough.

I didn't think he meant it as a criticism.

But when he walked into my apartment last night, he'd asked if I was renovating. He clearly thought my apart-ment needed renovating.

It shouldn't have been a huge surprise to me. Pretty much everyone who knew me had advised renovating at one point or another.

But back then, they'd suggested it to Nat. Nobody had suggested it to Tasha before. I was thinking this morning that Tasha might like to renovate.

Not that Tasha had the slightest idea of where to start.

But painting the walls seemed reasonable. With the right color of paint, you could make a huge difference without spending a lot of money.

I had hundreds of photos on my computer. I liked some of them a lot.

If I painted the wall, say, a nice cream or pale gold.

"Shut up, Nat," I said out loud.

Tasha, Tasha, Tasha, I thought inside my head. *What color do you like?*

It occurred to me to ask Jamie. After all, we'd agreed that he would trust my judgment and I would trust his. But after last night, I felt really weird about contacting him.

Then again, how better to make the first contact after our awkwardness than over something an innocuous as paint color? It was probably the perfect question: bland, lightweight, easy to answer.

I picked up my phone to type the text.

I'm painting my walls. What color should I use? Tasha.

Before I could talk myself out of it, I hit Send.
His text came back.

Your apartment?

I wasn't sure what other walls he thought I might be talking about.

Yes.

Shouldn't you be at work?

"Reasonable question," I muttered to myself as I typed.

I took a vacation day.

And you decided to paint?

Tasha is impulsive.

He sent a smiley face.

I'll have to come by and take a look.

The smiley face was nice. I felt like we'd made it past
the awkwardness. But the rest was disappointing.

I'd hoped he'd tell me mauve or burgundy or blue. I
was all set to head out to buy paint, brushes and a drop
sheet. I didn't want to sit here for the rest of the day and
think about redecorating. I wanted to get started.

I told myself I could clear the decks. Painting was
messy. I'd have to move the furniture to the middle of
the room. I should roll up the rugs. If I was moving the
furniture, I'd definitely need to vacuum underneath.

There was plenty I could do to get going.

I rose from the sofa, cleaned up the few breakfast
dishes and changed into some old jeans and a battered
sweatshirt.

The rugs were easy. I rolled them up and made a pile.

I decided I'd need about five feet in front of each wall.
That meant moving one sofa up against the coffee table.

It wouldn't be usable while I painted, but I wasn't planning on entertaining or anything.

I discovered I was right. Beneath the sofa there was quite an accumulation of dust and grit. I plugged in the vacuum and went to work. As it sucked up the debris, I studied the floor. It was in worse shape than the walls, all scratched and scuffed by about fifty years of students. If you looked closely, you could see the pattern of the desk rows, the little round dents from the desk legs and the worn paths where students trod in between.

I found myself smiling when I thought of all the kids that had learned in this room. When you thought about it, it was a nice provenance to have in a home. Maybe some of them had grown up to be doctors or pilots; maybe they were artists or athletes. I would bet a whole lot of them had kids and grandkids by now, Sunday barbecues and family baseball games.

I heard a noise and shut down the vacuum.

I waited, and it came again—a knock on the door.

My first thought was the downstairs neighbor. They were a young family with twin toddlers and a baby. My noise could be disturbing nap time.

I crossed to the door and opened it.

I was startled to see Jamie in the hall.

"What?" I asked, somehow not able to be more specific. "Weren't you downtown at the office?"

"I came to check out your walls."

"In the middle of the day?"

"You're playing hooky."

I found myself insulted at the accusation. "I put in for vacation leave. It's legit."

"I'm on an early lunch."

"It's ten thirty."

"Hence the word *early*. Are you going to let me in?"

"Sure." I stepped back. "Of course."

It occurred to me then how I looked. Not pretty, that was for sure. I hadn't bothered with makeup. I hadn't even showered yet today. My hair was in a quick knot on the top of my head. My gray sweatshirt was stained and boxy, and I had holes in the knees of my jeans.

I resisted the urge to smooth my hair or check my cheeks for streaks of dust. If Jamie was going to show up out of the blue, he got what he got. Tasha might dress up for a night on the town, but she dressed down for painting her apartment.

And, hey, I was painting my apartment. There should be points for that effort.

"I figured Jamie would duck out of the office if he had a good excuse."

"Jamie thinks picking my paint color is a good excuse?"

"I'm here to support you, Tasha," he said in a smooth, silky voice that trickled all the way through me.

I was *not* going to let things get awkward again.

I put some space between us.

"In that case, Jamie, what color should I use?"

He looked around for a long minute. He took a step, changed his angle, turned around.

"This really is…" he said.

"Utilitarian," I said.

He nodded. "That and a few other adjectives."

"Are you going to insult my apartment?"

He fought a smile. "I'm going to say Tasha's instincts are right. Paint is a good idea. Along with…" He looked around some more.

"I was wondering what to do with the floors," I said.

He looked down. "Fresh paint on the walls will definitely make the floors look tacky."

"I'd be offended, but I agree with you. It's high time I did something with this place."

I pictured Sophie for a moment. I had a feeling I was quoting her. She was going to be over the moon when she heard I was redecorating.

Trouble was, she'd want a hand in it. And she had very strong opinions.

I wanted this to be Tasha's apartment, not something tasteful and lovely that was inspired by Sophie.

I'd have to move fast. I wanted to be past the point of no return before Sophie dropped by and caught me.

"So," I said. "How adventurous do you think Tasha is feeling today?"

"Butter yellow with a russet-brown feature wall and some tangerine trim to make it pop."

"That sounds delicious," I said, trying to picture it.

"Maybe not tangerine," he said. "Maybe pumpkin. It's a bit darker."

"Do I want to know how you know all this?"

"I confess, I've wandered from the fashion blogs into home decorating a time or two."

I broke into a grin.

"It'll look great. I'm stealing it from a design I saw last week. I'll send it to you."

I did like the sounds of butter yellow. And given the size of the room and the walls, a contrasting wall seemed to make sense. I didn't know what pumpkin orange looked like, so who was I to say no?

"You could put stone laminate on the floor and pick up the colors."

I looked down.

I really liked the idea of a new floor. But I doubted I could afford it.

"I was thinking about something you said," Jamie said into the silence.

His words piqued my curiosity, and I looked up.

"You asked if Jamie would go with his gut, make a risky decision based on instinct."

I didn't want to argue again, so I didn't say anything.

"He would," Jamie said. "Oh, not on behalf of a client, that would be irresponsible. But he'd take a risk for himself. I'm sure of it."

He had me intrigued. "You're going to take a risk?"

"I think I should."

I saw the chance for a joke. "And you've thought this through."

He grinned at me. "Yes, I'm going to thoroughly analyze my instinctive, impulsive action."

"Do tell," I said. I backed up a little and folded myself into one of the armchairs, motioning for him to do the same.

He sat down across from me. "Short-term trading. High-risk, short-term trading with the potential for large financial gains."

"You're going to play the stock market."

It made sense for an economist, I supposed.

"*We're* going to play the stock market," he said.

I felt an immediate sinking sensation. "I don't have any money to lose."

"I'll stake us," he said. "We can share the profits."

That wasn't fair. "But—"

"No buts, Tasha."

"You're the one with the money. You're the one with the know-how." I would be dead weight in this.

"We'll make the decisions together. I'll explain my thinking to you, but we'll decide together. If it goes well, you'll be able to afford a new floor."

I looked to the ugly floor again. "I don't feel right about this."

Jamie came to his feet. "No, Nat doesn't feel right about this. Tasha thinks it's a great idea."

He was right, and I could tell by his expression he knew it.

Tasha, me, *I* was excited at the prospect of buying and selling stocks with Jamie, of having more secrets with Jamie, of spending more time with handsome, sexy, desirable Jamie.

Nat yelled stop. She recognized the danger.

But Tasha said go. She didn't need a reason.

Tasha won.

Seven

Rock wall climbing wasn't nearly as hard as I'd expected.

I'd have to learn the knots, and I'd have to learn how to put on a harness, and I'd have to learn a whole bunch of technical things before I'd be anywhere near ready to go out on my own. But the actual climbing, finding a handhold, finding a foothold, pulling myself toward the ceiling on the big vertical wall so far was a whole lot of fun.

I'd thought Jamie would be way, way better than me. Oh, he was definitely good, really good. But while he had bigger muscles, he also had a higher body mass to lift. Thanks to my short stature and relatively lean frame, I could hold my own.

I couldn't help but feel proud of that.

It also turned out that I had no fear of heights. I'd never given it much thought before, but quite a few of the people in the class got nervous as they climbed higher. As long as my harness was tight, I just enjoyed the view.

"You're a natural," Jamie said as my feet came down on the mat.

I was facing the wall, and he put his hands on my hips, obviously to make sure I stayed steady.

His touch felt good. It felt strong and secure. I didn't really want him to let me go.

"Your girlfriend's impressive," the instructor, Paul, said to Jamie.

Jamie abruptly let go. He seemed to realize how the gesture had looked.

I was glad my face was warm from exertion, or I might have worried about blushing. It wasn't such a huge mistake, thinking I was Jamie's girlfriend. After all, we'd signed up together. That would be perfectly natural.

As it was, Paul's suggestion embarrassed me. I might secretly want to be Jamie's girlfriend. In fact, I was starting to fantasize about it.

But that wasn't the point. The point here was to make Jamie attractive to other women. I was his sidekick, his means to an end, the person helping him replace Brooklyn with someone equally glamorous and exciting.

"Thanks," Jamie said to Paul.

I couldn't help but note that Jamie made no correction, offered no explanation, and was simply appreciative.

I felt stupidly good about that.

It didn't change anything. But for a second there, I felt more important to Jamie than just a pal. I liked that.

It would hurt later, I knew. But for the moment I was going to bask in the idea that someone, or maybe more than just Paul, considered Jamie and me a couple.

"Want to go up once more?" Paul asked me.

"Is there time for that?"

The clock was inching toward noon.

"Only for one of you," Paul said.

"Go ahead," Jamie said.

"You don't want to?" I didn't want to be greedy.

We'd each had three climbs this morning, after sitting through a presentation on theory and practicing some basic knots. I could see there was a whole lot to learn about the sport.

"Go ahead," Jamie said. "I'll watch Paul on belay."

I waited while Paul double-checked my ropes and equipment. Then I set off again, with Paul on the ground holding the rope to anchor me in case I slipped. To change things up, I started from a different point.

There were three climbers on the wall with me, each working with a different instructor.

Paul had told me to watch my feet. My feet were way more important than my hands. It made sense to me. And since I didn't have a ton of strength in my arms and shoulders—not being a regular at the gym or anything— I was more than happy to depend on my leg muscles. All that bike riding and running around on the tennis court was serving me well.

"Keep your arms straight," Paul called from below.

I reminded myself of that one, looking for a handhold farther away.

I saw one and took it, then I concentrated on my feet, finding the next step.

By the time I made it back down, my legs and arms were quivering. I knew I'd be sore tomorrow, but in a good way. This morning had been a whole lot of fun, and very satisfying.

Now, when I met new people at parties or anywhere really, and they asked my hobbies, I could sound daring and exciting. Who wouldn't be impressed with the answer *rock climbing* if they asked me what I did for fun? It was better than *tennis*, and sounded a whole lot more impressive than *reading*.

"Hungry?" Jamie asked as we drove from the parking lot in his SUV.

"I am. That really works up an appetite."

"Should we go watch some pretty people while we eat?"

"Where?"

"Northland Country Club. Have you ever been there?"

I had, but only once.

It was the high-end clubhouse at a private golf course. The restaurant was open to the public, but the prices were sky-high.

"Dressed like this?" I asked, knowing we'd never fit in.

"You look awesome."

"I look casual and sweaty."

He waved a dismissive hand as we pulled into traffic. "It's only lunchtime. Think of it as being incognito."

"No one will ever suspect we're spies?"

"Exactly. And it's on the way home."

"Sure," I said. "That sounds great."

There was no doubt that successful, stylish people frequented the Northland Country Club. It attracted business tycoons, politicians and millionaires from around the state and beyond.

"I hope our stock portfolio is rising," I said as we made our way through midday traffic. "I hear a cup of coffee costs sixteen dollars in that place."

Jamie tossed me his phone. "Check it out. The password is 8596."

I took a second to absorb the idea of Jamie giving me his password.

"You'll probably have to swipe over one screen. Open the Tracker app."

I entered the password, feeling like his girlfriend and telling myself to stop it already.

I swiped and tapped the app. Six lines came up with codes and numbers.

"What does it say?" he asked.

"CPW 27.32, LNN 2.06, QPP 32.17."

"Read that one again," he said.

"QPP?"

"Yes."

"QPP 32.17"

"Click on it."

I did.

"What do you see?"

"There's a graph."

"What does the trajectory look like?"

I didn't exactly understand the question.

"Long, slow start and sudden spike?" he asked.

"That's right."

"Hit the sell button."

I was kind of intimidated by the request. "Are you serious?"

"Completely. Go ahead."

"I'm selling stock?" I asked.

He grinned. "You are selling stock, Tasha."

"Okay." If he was sure, then I was game. I touched the sell button. "It's asking me to confirm."

"Confirm," he said.

I did. "Wow. That was exciting."

Jamie laughed.

"What did I just do?"

"You just paid for lunch."

"Really?" It felt pretty amazing.

"Lunch and a whole lot more," he said.

"How much did we make?"

"Ten percent."

"How much did we invest?"

"Ten thousand dollars."

I was speechless for a second. "That's... Jamie, we just made a thousand dollars?"

"I'm thinking champagne with lunch."

I looked back down at the phone. "But how...? It can't be that easy."

"It's not easy."

I felt like I'd insulted him, belittled his expertise and experience. "I know... I mean..."

The phone pinged in my hand and a text message came up. I automatically read it. "I'm sorry," I quickly said. "I didn't mean to pry."

"Who's it from?" he asked.

"Aaron."

"What did he say?"

"Are you sure you want me to—"

"You've already read it."

I couldn't tell if he was annoyed or not. "I didn't read it on purpose."

"I know that. What does it say?"

"It says Bernard postponed the IPO."

"Thank goodness," Jamie said.

"It's good?" I was glad it wasn't something to upset Jamie.

I wanted to go have lunch. I wanted to analyze beautiful people. I didn't want Jamie rushing off in a bad mood because of a problem at work.

"It means I talked them off the ledge. Aaron had their heads filled with ideas of quick riches and smooth sailing. It wasn't going to work that way."

"Maybe they should have thrown it all into QPP."

"There's nothing wrong with high risk when you're prepared to lose—whether it's a stock or an equity investment. I was prepared to lose on QPP. I doubt Bernard wants to risk losing control of his company."

"You were prepared to lose ten thousand dollars?" I couldn't wrap my head around that.

"We wouldn't have lost it all. Probably not. Likely not. But we could have lost some of it."

"You want me to read the rest of the numbers?" I asked, worried that we could be losing money on something else while we sat here talking.

"I'll check at lunch," he said. "For now, let's just bask in the win."

"Basking," I said as he swung into the country-club parking lot.

Once we'd cut in the edges, the painting went fast. Jamie was great with the roller, putting on an even coat. And with the roller extension, he could stand on the floor and paint all the way up to the high ceiling.

"What are we going to do up there?" he asked, looking at the ceiling.

I held on to the ladder and tipped my head. From up here, I could see more detail than I wanted to know about. "The skylights are really getting grungy."

"They definitely need to be replaced. Are they leaking?"

"No, thank goodness. Construction is way beyond my budget. I don't think the landlord would let me do it anyway."

"He would if it increased the value of his building."

"I suppose," I said.

"But he'd probably up your rent."

I went back to edging the russet-brown wall. I was on the last section cutting in the ceiling line.

"I'd have to get an agreement in advance," I said, thinking out loud.

"You should ask for a decrease in rent proportional with the amount you're putting into repairs."

"Would anyone go for that?"

It seemed like a good idea. But since I'd already started the work, I didn't see where I'd have leverage.

I could ask. I would ask. Maybe I wouldn't mention that I'd already done the painting.

"We should stop for the day," Jamie said.

I was tired, too. I met up with the final corner.

"I can't believe you did all this," I said, looking around.

The room looked brighter and fresher already.

We'd picked up the supplies after climbing yesterday, and Jamie had insisted on coming back to help me this morning.

I felt guilty then, and I felt even worse now, especially when I looked at my watch and saw that it was after six.

"We've been working for hours," I said.

He crossed the room and reached up toward me. "Hand me the paint can."

I bent over to get it to him. "I'm sorry I kept you all day."

He smiled, and his blue eyes warmed. At least, they warmed me. They warmed me a lot.

I had no idea whether or not he could tell.

Our hands brushed as I handed off the can, and the familiar charge of energy sped up my arm.

He looked sexy in his worn jeans, his faded T-shirt and scuffed work boots. I really liked the new scruffy look he seemed to have landed on. It emphasized his square chin, his strong, straight nose, his eyes that were honestly the most beautiful shade of blue. They were bright in the sun, midnight indoors, always startling, always striking.

His shoulders were broad under the snug shirt, his biceps taut and solid. Under a tux, he looked great. Dressed for construction, he looked spectacular.

"The brush," he prompted, pulling me out of my thoughts.

He was staring right at me, into my expression, into my eyes, and for a terrible second I thought he could read my mind. If he could see my thoughts, he'd know I was compromised. I wasn't his buddy, his pal, his wingman.

I was falling for him. And that wasn't even remotely what he'd signed up for here. He'd be disappointed if he knew. He might even be amused if he knew. Mousy little Nat Remington thought a veneer of makeup and a few new clothes would turn her into Brooklyn.

Sure.

Could happen.

In my dreams.

I leaned down to give him the paintbrush.

The ladder shifted. The brush slipped from my fingers.

The russet-brown end caught Jamie in the forehead. "Crap!" I cried out. The brush bounced to the floor. Jamie grasped the ladder, righting it, but dislodging me.

I lost my balance and fell into his arms, and he caught me, pulling me tight before my feet hit the floor.

The ladder wasn't so fortunate. It teetered, then tipped, then banged on the linoleum, the sound reverberating.

"Good thing we moved the paint can," he said.

I blew out a sigh of relief. "You caught me."

"I caught you," he said.

He shifted, and our gazes met.

They locked.

His arms flexed tight around me.

We stared at each other in silence while time suspended.

"Tasha," he whispered.

I wanted him.

I wanted to breathe him, to taste him, to feel him touch me anywhere and everywhere.

I was about to make a fool of myself.

If he didn't let me go, I was going to kiss him hard and long, and he'd know exactly how I'd been feeling all these days.

He kissed me.

Okay, that was unexpected.

I hadn't seen it going that way at all.

But there it was.

His lips were on mine. They were firm and tender and delicious, and this was the best kiss of my life, possibly the best kiss ever in the history of mankind.

I didn't want it to stop.

I cupped his cheeks, feeling the stubble like I'd been dying to do since he'd grown it out.

It felt rough and rugged, adding to my sensory overload.

My breasts were pressed against his chest, my thighs against his, my belly, his belly, his sex.

A roaring sound came up in my ears, as the kiss went on and on and on.

He pulled off my T-shirt, revealing my lacy bra.

We stared at each other, breathing hard. I think we were trying to figure out which of us was more shocked.

Only I wasn't shocked. Okay, I was shocked. But I was aroused more than shocked. I was aroused more than anything.

He removed my glasses. I peeled off his shirt, for the first time getting a look—though it was blurry—at his magnificent pecs, his bare shoulders, what I knew were gorgeous abs.

He reached for the clasp of my bra, and I knew we

were gone. This was right out of control, and we weren't stopping for anything.

My doorknob rattled.

We simultaneously whipped our heads in that direction.

"Nat?" It was Sophie.

She knocked. "Nat? I can hear your music. Is everything okay?"

"She has a key," I hissed to Jamie.

He set me down.

I grabbed my T-shirt from the tipped ladder and threw it over my head.

"I'm coming," I called to her.

Jamie threw on his own T-shirt and ran his fingers through his hair.

We stared at each other for a second.

I had no idea what to say or do or even think.

We'd almost had sex.

I gave myself a shake and went for the door.

"What took you so long?" Sophie said as she marched in.

"I was up on the ladder," I said.

She saw Jamie first. Then she saw the ladder and the painted walls.

I could almost hear her brain humming as she took everything in.

"Hi, Sophie," Jamie said.

"What?" Sophie seemed at a loss for words as she looked around.

"James was helping me paint."

Sophie looked completely confused. "Why would he do that?"

As far as Sophie knew, Jamie and I barely talked to each other—which had always been true in the past.

"We were talking, uh, the other day," I said, my mind scrambling for something logical.

"At the tennis club," Jamie put in.

"Yes," I said. "At the tennis club. And I was asking, well, you know, all the stuff you and Bryce and Ethan told me." I went with the first and only thing that came into my mind—Sophie's new business. "And with James's job and all. Well, it got me to thinking, maybe, and I didn't want to say anything to you, because it wouldn't be fair. You know, if it didn't work out."

Sophie and Jamie were both staring at me as if I'd lost my mind.

Which I had. I apparently had completely lost my mind.

To be fair, my brain had overheated from Jamie's kiss.

After a kiss like that, a woman shouldn't be required to think anything coherent for at least a couple of hours, maybe all night long.

"Ethan was saying you needed investors," I plowed on. "James sometimes invests in things. So, I asked him." I looked at Jamie, trying to apologize with my eyes. "I asked him about your 3-D printer dessert thing, if it was maybe something that he could invest in."

"You did?" Sophie looked amazed and hopeful at the same time.

"But I don't think it's going to work out," I quickly said. "It's not the kind of thing that—"

"I'm going to need more information," Jamie said.

I gave him a warning look. My story was only a way to get us through this awkward moment. We couldn't let it go any further.

Sophie moved closer to where Jamie was standing. "We can give you anything you want."

"James usually makes short-term investments," I said

from behind her, trying to shut it down. "Yours is at a really early stage. And it's going to take a long, long time."

"We're going to revolutionize the food service industry," Sophie said.

My gaze hit Jamie's, half apology, half warning.

"We're upping the level of precision and sophistication with which restaurants," Sophie said before I could slow her down, "even small establishments, can conceive, refine, create and serve desserts of all kinds with our technology."

What had I done?

"That was amazing," Sophie said, dropping down on the single sofa that wasn't covered by the painting drop sheets. "But why was James here? And why are you renovating? And why didn't you tell me?"

I decided to answer the easiest question. "It was a sudden decision."

"I could have helped. I can still help. What's your color scheme? What else are you doing besides the walls?"

I said a silent thank-you that we'd moved past James.

I pushed the passionate kiss from my mind. Could I call it a kiss? It was a whole lot more than a kiss—even if we hadn't technically gone any further than a kiss.

"Butter yellow." I did a circle point to the painted walls. "Plus a russet-brown feature wall. And we're… I'm thinking of adding some pumpkin accents."

Sophie stared unblinking at me. "Who are you and what have you done with my friend Nat?"

I wanted to say I was Tasha. But I kept the thought inside my head.

I did smile.

Sophie smiled back. "This is going to be fun."

I'd known that one would be coming.

"Have you thought about furniture?" she asked. "It would be so much fun shopping. This stuff is pretty tatty."

"I'll have to check my budget before I decide."

"It doesn't have to be right away. I mean, not all of it anyway. We can start with some small pieces. Honestly, Nat, anything would be an improvement."

"You keep telling me that."

"And you're finally *doing* it." She grinned. "We need to celebrate."

Then she went quiet for a moment, looking thoughtful.

I braced myself for another question about James. I hoped I could keep a straight face and that I wouldn't have to lie too much. I wasn't going to betray Jamie's confidence. But I was thinking I could talk a little bit about the changes I'd made to my own image—my hair, my contacts, my apartment.

People upgraded their lives all the time. It wasn't so weird.

"Do you think he'll do it?" Sophie asked.

I was guessing she meant Jamie.

"He said he'd talk to people," she continued. "I guess he must know those kinds of people. He works in a financial place, right?"

"He does." I didn't want to say more. I didn't want to get her hopes up.

It was impossible to tell if Jamie was being polite and trying to protect my cover story, or if he really did know people he could talk to about angel investment into a tech start-up company.

I would have liked to ask him—about the money, about the kiss. At least, I thought I'd like to ask him about the kiss.

It had been one incredible kiss. We'd practically torn off each other's clothes. We had chemistry together. That was for sure.

But I was nervous because this wasn't what Jamie had signed up for. And it could have been a momentary impulse. Physical attraction could take you by surprise, and he might regret it already.

The best thing to do was to take his lead. That made sense to me. If he wanted to talk about it, we'd talk about it. If he wanted to pretend it never happened, I'd go along with that.

I didn't want to mess up our friendship or our deal to help each other. Both had become too important to me.

"Nat?" Sophie said. "What do you think?"

I ordered myself to stop obsessing. It was a kiss. It was over. Life was moving on.

"I don't want you to be disappointed," I said to her. It was my honest answer.

"I can't help but be hopeful. I should really call Ethan."

I was surprised Ethan was her first thought. "What about Bryce?"

"Oh, him, too. Of course, him, too. But Ethan's put his heart and soul into this. Bryce is a little bit on the sidelines with the recipes and all."

That hadn't been my impression. Bryce had seemed quite passionate about the project.

"We should meet them somewhere," Sophie said.

"It's Sunday night."

"It's not even eight o'clock. We can grab dinner and talk about the possibilities. Whatever happens, we should be prepared for it."

If I had to make a bet, I'd say nothing was going to come of this. And I really didn't feel like going out right now.

I made a show of looking down at myself. "I'm a mess."

"We won't go anywhere fancy. Comb you hair, put on some makeup, change your clothes."

That all sounded like a whole lot of work to me. I was exhausted.

"Angelo's at the Lake would be perfect. It's only five minutes from here."

"I'm really tired," I said. "And I have to work tomorrow."

"Come on, Nat. This is huge. I mean, I know it's not a sure thing. But I want to see Ethan's face when I tell him the news."

"There's no news yet," I pointed out.

"You have to eat," she said. "Summon up that peppy new gal who did all this redecorating and come out for dinner with your best friend."

When she put it that way, I felt like a cad saying no.

"Fine," I said.

Her grin made me feel a little more energized.

I pushed myself from the depths of the comfy armchair, telling myself I'd perk up once I got out in the fresh air.

While I got myself ready, Sophie texted Ethan and Bryce.

I combed out my hair, fighting a few globs of stubborn paint. It occurred to me that I should have worn a hat while I painted. I'd definitely do that next time.

I washed my face, brushed my teeth, and put on a little makeup before changing into black jeans and a dove-gray sweater with a silver thread running through the weave. The jeans were a gift from Brooklyn. They were tighter than the ones I usually bought, so I hadn't worn them often. But I was feeling very Tasha-y right now.

"They'll meet us there," Sophie called out.

"Okay," I called back.

I put a pair of silver hoops in my ears and decided I was ready.

I did feel a little more energized. And I was really hungry. Angelo's made fantastic seafood lasagna. I was going to treat myself to that.

I felt bad that I hadn't fed Jamie. I'd planned on ordering something in once we'd cleaned up. As it was, all I'd done was close the paint can and put the brushes and roller to soak while Jamie had talked to Sophie about investments.

"I'm all set," I said as I walked around the divider.

"That was fast." Sophie did a double take of me and then stared.

"What?" I asked, looking down at myself and craning my neck to see the back.

"You look great," she said.

"Thanks."

"No really… I mean…you look… Wow."

"I'm going to assume that's good."

Sophie took in her own outfit of blue jeans and a multicolored blouse. "I feel like I should change."

Her hair was windblown, and her makeup wasn't as fresh as it usually was, but she looked perfectly good.

"Don't be silly," I said. "You look awesome. It's not like you need to impress Bryce. He's impressed already."

I wasn't an expert on long-term relationships. My romance with Henry Paulson didn't qualify, since it had crashed and burned. But it seemed to me that at some point you could start relaxing your look around your boyfriend.

I thought about how I'd looked today with Jamie. I'd looked pretty casual, beyond casual. I'd looked downright functional—probably because I *was* downright functional.

Not that Jamie and I had anything romantic going.

Even that kiss hadn't been romantic. It had been passionate and erotic and exciting. But I wasn't foolish enough to equate those things with romantic.

Sophie still looked uncertain.

"You want to borrow some makeup?" I asked. "I'd offer my wardrobe, but you know what my clothes are like."

Sophie laughed at that. "That's a cute outfit, though."

"These are the jeans Brooklyn gave me last year."

"Oh, yeah. I remember. Why don't you wear them more often?"

"They're a bit snug."

"They fit perfect. You've got to get away from the early-matron look."

"I think you mean the early-librarian look." I was trying to get away from it.

It occurred to me that I should do some more shopping. Maybe Jamie would like to come with me. Maybe I was obsessing about Jamie. Maybe I should get a grip.

"Either." Sophie paused. "I think I will borrow a little mascara or something."

"Help yourself." I gestured to the bathroom.

While she was gone, I opened the closet and took in my shoe choices.

The black cutout ankle boots I'd bought for the dance club would go great with the jeans. I hesitated, knowing I would have to explain them to Sophie.

But I couldn't resist.

I put them on. Then I stood in front of my full-length mirror.

I looked sharp. I had that casual, "I don't really care about it, but I look pretty great" appearance that Brooklyn seemed to so effortlessly achieve.

Part of me was excited, and part of me couldn't truly believe it was me staring back from the mirror.

Eight

Jamie agreed to another shopping trip.

But there was something off in his texts. They were so brief and to the point. He seemed more formal somehow than usual. And then I thought I was imagining it. And then I thought I was still obsessing about the kiss—which I was—and I was reading things into his seven-word texts that simply weren't there.

After work on Wednesday, one of my coworkers dropped me off downtown. Jamie and I had agreed to meet at Brookswood. We'd barely scratched the surface of its ten floors when we bought his tux and my dress.

I'd decided to blow the clothing budget today. Our investment account profits were still climbing. I'd told Jamie quite a few times that it felt wrong for me to share in the profits, since he'd provided the seed money, and since it was his expertise making the trades.

But he wouldn't listen. He said he'd already made back the seed money and a deal was a deal. I was getting my half.

I'd given up fighting.

If he was going to insist, then I supposed I'd accept

it. I pictured myself Christmas shopping this year with a lavish budget and so many choices to surprise my family and friends.

And maybe I'd buy a couple of fancy outfits. Or maybe some not-so-fancy outfits. I could buy some of those deceptively casual clothes that were high quality and well made. To other people, they simply looked good. The secret was that they made *you* look good.

I was beginning to realize that Brooklyn and Sophie were onto something. There was a difference in quality and flair as you moved up the price range. Sometimes it seemed subtle, but it was real.

Last Sunday when I wore the black jeans to Angelo's, a dozen guys turned their heads when I walked to the ladies' room. Nobody had pointed, at least not that I saw. But many of them had followed me along, appreciative gazes on their faces.

Ironically, Ethan hadn't been one of them. Although Sophie kept trying, Ethan and I were never going to connect.

He connected better with Sophie than he did with me. I supposed that had a lot to do with their business venture. But still, his expression lit up for her and stayed flat for me.

Sometimes I thought Bryce saw that. Sometimes I thought Bryce got annoyed.

Sophie seemed like the only one who didn't notice.

After the outing at Angelo's, I vowed that if she suggested another double date, I was going to be frank with her and refuse. I wanted to spend girl time with Sophie. I wanted to hear more about her business venture. It was obvious she was really excited about that. But I hoped I could do it without spending another uncomfortable evening with Ethan.

I could tell Ethan had a crush on her. But I didn't want

to throw that kind of a grenade into the Sweet Tech business venture. If Bryce didn't want to address it, there was no value in me addressing it. I would probably make things worse by telling her.

Jamie beat me to Brookswood and was waiting outside the main door.

"Hi," I said, feeling suddenly breathless.

He looked sexy, handsome and aloof.

"Hi," he said back and immediately turned for the door.

He held it open for me and I once again entered the rarefied environment of high-end shopping.

After a few steps, I opened the conversation. "Did you have a nice day?"

"It was fine." His strides were long and I had to hurry to keep up.

"So was mine."

"Good. Do you want to start with office wear, casual wear, a jacket? The weather's going to turn soon."

The weather? We were going to talk about the weather?

"Jamie?"

"Hmm?"

"What's going on?"

He looked down at me. But he wasn't seeing me, not really.

"What?" he asked.

"Something's wrong. What's wrong?"

"Nothing. We're shopping. You're right. We both need a more extensive new wardrobe. I hope you're not planning to bargain hunt."

"I'm not. You've convinced me to spend the investment profits. At least, you've convinced Tasha to spend the investment profits. Turns out she's not as scrupulous as me."

I expected him to laugh at my joke, but he didn't.

"You are Tasha," he said.

"You know what I mean."

"And it's not unscrupulous to spend money that belongs to you. What about shirtdresses? I read they're a thing."

"Jamie, stop."

He clamped his jaw, but he stopped.

"Look at me."

He turned, the aloof expression firmly in place.

"Is it the kiss?" I asked, tired of feeling jumpy, tired of trying to guess how he felt about it.

From the way he was acting, I could definitely guess he regretted it.

I pushed myself forward. "Are you being like this because we kissed each other?"

He didn't answer. And he sure didn't look happy that I'd brought it up.

I wanted to let him off the hook, to show him it was no big deal and I hadn't been obsessing about it—which, of course, I had, like every second since it happened.

"It was a kiss," I said. "A simple kiss. People do that. We were working together. We were happy. Plus, we've been, you know, turning each other into the image we think will attract the opposite sex." As I framed up my explanation, I decided it was pretty good. "All that kiss meant was that it's working. It's working, and that's a good thing. Hey, you should have seen the guys react to me at Angelo's on Sunday night."

Jamie sucked in a breath.

So did I. I needed oxygen to keep on talking. "They liked my look. A lot of them liked my look. As for you and me, well, it would be weird if we weren't a little bit attracted to each other. Don't you think that's true? And we were. And we kissed. And it's over. It doesn't have to mean a thing. It doesn't have to make you go all…" I gestured up and down at his posture. "I don't know, James-the-uptight on me."

"I'm not uptight." But he said it through teeth that were kind of clenched.

"I doesn't have to mean anything," I repeated. "It doesn't have to change anything. I don't want it to change anything."

I really, really didn't want anything to change between us, and I was afraid that I'd already blown it. These past few weeks had been the most enlightening, exciting and downright fun of my life. I didn't want to lose Jamie, and I desperately hoped my unbridled reaction to his kiss hadn't done just that.

He stayed silent for a moment. "It didn't change anything."

I felt a tiny hint of relief. "Then smile or something."

He tried, but it didn't come off.

I decided to keep it light and hope against hope that tactic would work. "Well, that's pathetic. The Jamie I know would blow past a little kiss in a heartbeat."

"You call that a little kiss?" he asked.

"I do."

We stared at each other for a moment.

He seemed to be daring me to do something or say something. But I couldn't tell what he wanted.

I took a stab. "I want to stay friends, Jamie. I really don't want to lose what we have."

His expression finally relaxed just a little bit. "Neither do I."

"Good." I was relieved, and I was glad. I didn't dare say anything more.

Instead, I glanced past him to the racks behind. "I don't really want a shirtdress."

"No shirtdress then," he said. "How about a jacket?"

I wouldn't say the shopping trip was the best time we'd ever had. We were still tippy-toeing around each other.

But at least it was successful. We both left the store with armloads of new clothes, shoes and some jewelry for me.

Jamie got a text while we were paying and asked if I minded stopping at his office.

I easily agreed, not yet feeling like we were back on normal ground.

We drove over and parked in the company garage in a spot labeled for Jamie.

His key fob opened the doors, and an elevator whisked us to the thirty-second floor.

Aaron was sitting at a desk in the open office area.

There were a couple of other people in the distance, but otherwise the office was empty and quiet.

"Tell me exactly what Bernard said," Jamie said to Aaron.

"You didn't have to come all the way in," Aaron said.

"I assume it was you who changed his mind."

"A lot of things changed his mind. He thought about it, and he decided he's willing to take the chance."

"He never should have been put in this predicament in the first place. Watch and learn, Aaron. How hard is it to understand the concept of watch and learn?"

Jamie was angry.

I didn't know what to do with myself.

I felt awful just standing here listening to the argument, but there wasn't an easy way for me to escape. It was a long walk back to the elevators, and I wasn't sure where I would go from there. All the offices around the periphery of the space were closed. Not that I'd randomly walk into somebody's office.

"Rehashing it isn't going to help," Aaron said in obvious frustration.

Jamie clenched his jaw. "Then give me a path forward. You set this up. What's your solution?"

Aaron stood. "It's done, so we roll with it."

Jamie coughed out a laugh. "Go public on Monday without doing due diligence?"

"It's going to work, James." Aaron's tone was emphatic now. "I know in my gut that it's going to work."

"We're not trusting your gut. Your gut's only two months old."

"What about your gut?" Aaron asked.

The question seemed to throw Jamie.

"What does your gut tell you?"

I could see that Jamie didn't want to answer. I had to wonder if it was because he disagreed with Aaron or because he agreed with Aaron.

For some reason, he looked at me.

I tried to give him an encouraging smile, even though I had no idea what he was thinking.

The last thing he might want is for me to be happy when he was so obviously frustrated.

I wasn't happy about his frustration, of course.

But I was curious about the obvious struggle going on inside his head.

"I'm not recording this," Aaron said.

Jamie glared at him.

"Gut reaction." Aaron shrugged. "What could it hurt to say it out loud?"

"It'll work," Jamie said.

"There we go." Aaron smiled.

"No, there we *don't* go."

"Do you want me to explain gut reactions to you?" Aaron asked.

"No," Jamie drawled. "I do *not* want you to explain gut reactions to me."

"They're made up of subtle signals, information that

you don't even know you know. It happens deep in your subconscious."

"What part of *no* did you miss?"

"It's not your gut working, James. It's your brain, your whole brain, the deep recesses of your entire brain. You know the answer. You just don't like working without the data on paper, driving without a seat belt."

"Jumping without a parachute," Jamie said. "And I change my mind all the time based on the data on paper."

"How do you do the short-term stuff?" I asked.

I thought I was being helpful, but Jamie shot me the same glare as he'd shot Aaron.

I wasn't being helpful.

"That's completely different," he said. "You know that. I explained that."

He had.

But I didn't see it being completely different. Then again, what did I know? I was a librarian, not an economist.

"Sorry," I said. I was.

"Bernard will ask for our recommendation in the morning," Aaron said.

Seconds ticked by.

"What do we say?" Aaron asked.

More seconds ticked by. I thought Jamie wasn't going to answer.

"Recommend the IPO," he said. His tone made the words sound painful.

"All right!" Aaron shouted and made a fist.

"Don't get cocky," Jamie said. "And if this goes bad…"

"It's on me." Aaron nodded.

"No, it's on me. Because that's the way it works."

Now I was nervous. I hated to think I might have pushed Jamie toward a decision he wasn't comfortable with.

"Jamie, if you're not—"

"Relax, Tasha. You didn't talk me into anything."

I swallowed.

Aaron spoke up. "The mighty James Gillen isn't one to take his girlfriend's advice."

Jamie's tone was cutting. "You don't know whose advice I'll take."

Then he turned to me. He looked tired, and his voice lost its edge. "Come on, Tasha. I'll drive you home."

Rock climbing training was uneventful on Saturday. It felt like our relationship was somewhat back on an even keel, and I told myself to be happy about that.

I didn't have any plans for Saturday night. I was disappointed that I wouldn't get to take any of my new, new clothes out for a test-drive. I'd bought this dusty blue tufted blouse and a short, blotchy, dusty-blue-and-pink-patterned skirt that I was dying to wear somewhere. It was set off with a wide black satin sash, and I'd bought oversize pearl earrings and a necklace to go with it.

It was softly romantic, and totally not me. I wasn't completely sure it was Tasha either, but I was willing to give it a shot. Both the salesclerk at Brookswood and Jamie had said it was a "must."

Who was I to say no to a "must"?

But it wasn't going to be this weekend.

I told myself it was just as well. I still had a lot of work to do on my apartment. If I pushed myself I could get the pumpkin—it turned out that was a very popular color—trim done today. Then I could put my furniture back and feel normal again.

Well, the new normal, of course.

I really did like the way the paint was turning out. It felt fresh and alive. I found it energizing to be at home.

If I worked hard, I'd be ready to start on the floors. I'd already picked up samples of stone and wood laminate. Not all of the brands were expensive, especially if you shopped carefully.

I liked the stone patterns best. It gave you the greatest range of color options.

So, Sunday morning, I dressed in paint clothes. I'd picked up a white cap at the hardware store, and I folded my hair underneath. I wasn't going to risk globs of pumpkin orange in my hair.

I'd masked stripes on the top and bottom of the walls, plus a wide box around each window.

I shook the paint bucket, pried it open, gave it a stir and then held my breath.

The butter yellow and russet brown were pretty lowrisk colors. The orange on the other hand was going to pop. I felt like that first stroke was a momentous decision.

There was a knock on my door.

I gave myself a split second to wonder if it was a sign. Maybe I wasn't supposed to paint bright orange on my walls.

The knock came again.

I balanced the brush across the top of the open can, half-relieved by the interruption and half-annoyed that I was being given a chance to change my mind. I didn't want to change my mind. I wanted to dive wholeheartedly into my new bright orange life.

I opened the door to find Jamie standing there with two coffees and a paper bag from Penelope's Bakery.

His appearance took me by surprise. When he'd said goodbye yesterday he didn't say anything about helping me again. Not that I wouldn't say yes to the help. I'd really appreciate it.

Then again, he might not be here to help at all. He

could be here for something completely unrelated to my apartment renovations. I shouldn't be so presumptuous.

"Hungry?" he asked.

"Why are you here?" I sounded rude. "I mean, sure, yes, I'm hungry."

He rattled the bag. "Fresh bagels."

I realized I hadn't eaten breakfast.

"I was just starting to paint," I said.

"Then I'm right on time." He moved forward, and I got out of the way.

"I didn't know you were coming," I said as I closed the door.

I was positive he hadn't said anything yesterday.

"Spur-of-the-moment. I stopped by Penelope's. The blueberry bagels made me think of you."

"Blueberry bagels? Really?" I couldn't for the life of me see the connection.

"Okay, it was the giant éclair in the refrigerated case. It reminded me of that time at the Orchid Club."

I remembered the decadent dessert we'd shared on that first reconnaissance foray outside the Orchid Club. We'd ordered mini cream puffs drizzled with chocolate and caramel sauce. I'd eaten the lion's share, and Jamie had teased me about my enthusiasm.

"But I thought it might be a bit much for breakfast, so I went with the bagels."

"Too bad," I said, only half joking.

Chocolate and pastry cream was my weakness.

"I can go back," he said.

"No, probably a good call. I don't want to go into a sugar coma before I finish painting."

Jamie handed me one of the coffee cups and looked around. "Seems like you're all set to go."

I decided coffee and fresh bagels would be worth the

delay in starting. I took one end of the uncovered sofa that was angled in the middle of the room.

Jamie sat on the other end and put the bag of bagels between us.

"I'm hoping to finish today," I said.

Then I remembered the flooring samples and hopped back up, going to the kitchen counter where I'd left them.

"Take a look at these," I said as I carried them over to him.

Jamie had opened the bag and extracted a bagel. Both his hands were occupied.

"After you finish," I said and helped myself to a bagel.

"You've inspired me," he said.

"With flooring samples?" I grinned as I took a bite. It was awesome. "Mmm."

"With your willingness to change your life," he said.

It wasn't all me. It was far from all me.

I swallowed. "You're changing yours just as much."

He shook his head. "Not as much. Not everything."

"What do you mean?"

"I mean I need a new house."

I gave another big swallow. Okay, that was pretty huge.

"Are you sure? I mean, we only paid a couple hundred dollars for the paint." As commitments went, sweat equity wasn't nearly as serious as a mortgage.

"I'm moving up," Jamie said. "Or I'm moving sideways. I mean, I'm moving to where Jamie wants to live."

"Do we know where Jamie wants to live?" I asked.

"We're going to find out."

"Wow. That's huge."

"I'm counting on your help."

The statement, along with his expression, made me nervous. My head started to shake all on its own. "I'm not picking out your house."

"You did a terrific job with my car."

My head shaking continued. "That's crazy. It's nuts. A house is a major life decision, maybe *the* major life decision. It's a huge, long-term commitment. You have to pick it out yourself."

"I checked our stock portfolio this morning." He paused. It seemed like he was going for dramatic effect.

I wasn't sure if I should take that as a good or a bad thing. Good, I had to think, if he was talking about it in conjunction with buying a house.

Then again, I didn't want to get my hopes up. He'd come up with the investment seed money without too much trouble. He probably also had a decent down payment waiting in the wings. The two things might have nothing to do with each other.

"And…" I prompted.

"And it's up."

"Good." I was relieved—more for Jamie than for me.

I didn't really have anything at stake in it. We'd already taken out the money for our clothes-buying binge. But Jamie still had his capital at risk. I knew that stocks could fall just as easily as they could rise. And we'd had an awfully good run of it lately.

"Way up," he said.

I could tell he was toying with me.

"Are we going to play this game all morning?" I asked.

He grinned. "Remember Street Wrangle, the wireless company?"

I did. "Yes."

"Remember how I said they'd inexplicably bought that property next to Newmister?"

I remembered that, too. Jamie had speculated that the companies might be talking about a merger.

"They merged?" I asked.

There was a light in Jamie's eyes that said this was big. I lost interest in my bagel.

"They merged. The stock spiked. It's set to split first thing Monday morning. Traders are lining up to get in. I've never seen buzz like this."

"But we're already in."

Jamie held his coffee cup up in a toast. "We're already in."

"Did we invest a lot?"

"We were bold. We went with our gut."

My grin grew, feeling like it might split my cheeks. "Oh, I *do* like Jamie's audacity."

"Will you help me find a house?"

"I'm scared." This situation called for me to be completely honest.

"Don't be scared."

"I don't know the first thing about real estate. I'll screw it up."

"You won't screw it up."

I gave a chopped laugh of disbelief. There were a thousand ways for me to screw up a choice like this—from location to plumbing to the foundation to...well, everything.

"Don't be scared, Tasha," he said in the gentlest of tones. "You're smart and methodical. And you have great instincts. You have gut instincts that are incredibly impressive. Run with them. Be audacious." He paused and seemed to be thinking. "Plus, I love your taste. You know you found me a great vehicle. Look at it this way, I just moved into a whole new housing bracket." He smiled and reached out to give my hand a quick squeeze. "This is going to be *fun*."

I considered his words. They were heartwarming.

I was on my way to being convinced, but I wasn't quite

there. "You have a warped idea of fun. This is going to be *stressful*."

"No, stressful is slapping pumpkin on a freshly painted wall and hoping it looks okay."

"Wait a minute. You were the one who picked out the orange paint."

"And you let me. That was very trusting of you."

"This is on you," I said.

I took a last bite of bagel.

"I'll take that risk." Jamie finished his bagel and tipped back his coffee.

We stowed the trash. Then we crouched down at opposite ends of a wall and started painting orange.

Four hours later, our paintbrushes met in the middle of the last window.

We both straightened up. We took a few backward steps and gazed around.

I was amazed.

It looked fantastic.

"How did you know?" I asked him.

"Know what?"

"That it would look this good?"

"I cheated," he said.

"Cheated how?"

"I stole the idea from a decorating website, remember?"

"Nice steal." I couldn't believe this stylish, sophisticated apartment was mine. Now I couldn't wait to get going on the flooring.

Nine

"If you can do this without flinching," Jamie said to me as we stared up the thirty-foot rock face, "then you can definitely pick me out a house."

We'd looked at three different houses on Thursday night. While I'd tried to drag Jamie's opinion out of him, he kept insisting it was my choice to make. I'd been afraid to say I liked anything for fear he'd pull out his checkbook right then and there.

"I can do *this* without flinching," I said. I was excited about our climb, not frightened.

Spending hundreds of thousands of someone else's dollars? Now, *that* was frightening.

We were on a field trip with Paul, the other instructors and the rest of our class. It was a graduation ceremony of sorts, although Jamie and I had already signed up for the next level of climbing class, as had most of the rest of the class. We weren't qualified to undertake more than an uphill hike or a scramble by ourselves at this point.

"Great," Jamie said.

"But you really do have to weigh in on the house."

We'd seen two more houses last night with the Realtor Emily-Ann. I'd liked the last one quite a lot.

"Go through your safety check," the head instructor called out.

I made sure my watch was zipped into my pocket. I checked my harness buckles, my leg loops, rope orientation and carabiner. Jamie and I double-checked each other's knots, then we waited for Paul to give us a thumbs-up. We both passed his check, and we were ready to go.

I was going first with Jamie on belay.

Each of three teams had chosen a different section of the rock face.

I was ready.

I was excited.

"On belay?" I called back to Jamie.

"On belay," he confirmed.

"Climbing," I called.

"Climb on," he answered.

I found my first foothold, flexing my toe. I'd learned most of the patterns on the climbing wall, and it was exciting to be trying something completely new.

I was connected by a top rope that looped from the top of the climb back to Jamie. I trusted Jamie, and Paul was supervising, so I focused on the foot- and handholds.

I dead-ended once and had to back down a few steps, but otherwise, I made it up without any mistakes.

When I looked back down, Jamie was beaming and giving me a clap.

He lowered me down, and I took belay while he climbed.

By the end of the morning, we were all stripping off our windbreakers under the beaming sun. Paul and the other instructors had brought along a light picnic and some celebratory champagne.

Jamie and I toasted each other in the fresh air, laughing at our accomplishments.

He pulled me into an unexpected hug.

I felt arousal buzz through me.

"Now, that was adventure," he whispered in my ear.

"We are wild and exciting," I whispered back.

"Who wouldn't want to point at us across a room?" he asked.

"Or fall madly in love with us?"

His hug tightened for a second.

"Anyone who wants to take the long way home…" the head instructor said in a loud voice. Then he pointed. "There's a trail from here that goes around the face. It leads to a viewpoint lookout. Farther up, you can get into Pebble Pond. Then the main trail loops around back to the parking lot."

"It's all about the views," Paul said.

Most people were shaking their heads. Everyone was already hot and tired.

Jamie drew back to look at me.

"Game?" he asked.

I was.

In the end, six of us changed into hiking shoes and walked the two miles to the viewpoint.

As Paul had said, the view was spectacular, sweeping green hillsides, spikes of evergreens, and snowcapped peaks surrounding a deep blue lake in the valley bottom.

The rest of the group turned around there.

Jamie wanted to keep going, and my exhilaration was giving me energy. I felt like I could hike all day.

My exhilaration was ebbing by the time we made it along the narrow path to Pebble Pond.

The picturesque and isolated spot was worth the hike,

but I'd admit I was glad we'd be going downhill on the way back.

"I like this," Jamie said, gazing out at the blue-green water surrounded by towering rocks and lush grasses and shrubs. A few cedars clustered near one shore with a group of crows circling the tops, calling to one another in the silent wind.

We were on a tiny stretch of pebble-covered beach. The smooth little rocks were quite a pretty mix of white, blue gray, amber, green and black. Some were solid colors. Some were striped. And some were mottled. It was easy to see how the pond got its name.

It felt like we were all alone in the world.

Above us, an eagle took flight from the cedar trees, then another followed, chasing off the crows.

"Nature in the raw," I said, quoting something I'd once heard.

"My money's on the eagles," Jamie said.

"They must have a nest up there. Chicks do you think?"

"It seems late in the season. But they look like they're guarding something."

The eagles swooped in tandem, and the crows scattered.

The world fell silent again with the barest of breezes lifting the leaves around us.

"I'm sweltering," Jamie said.

I guessed the sun was reflecting off the surrounding rock faces. We did seem to be in a pocket of still heat.

Jamie stripped off his shirt.

My mouth went dry, and my brain paused for a beat. To be fair, I was dying of thirst. But the brain seize was all Jamie—his abs looked like they'd been sculpted from marble. His pecs and shoulders were firm, smooth and rounded. His biceps bulged, and his forearms were thick and sturdy.

I knew he had strong hands. I'd watched him work. But they looked stronger against the backdrop of nature.

Then he reached for the button of his khakis.

"Wh-what are you doing?" My stutter was mortifying.

"Taking a dip," he said, and dragged down his zipper. "Aren't you hot?"

I was hot. I was very hot. I was a whole lot hotter than I'd been two minutes ago.

"Don't look so worried," he said. "I'm not getting naked or anything. Come in with me. You're wearing underwear, aren't you?"

I was wearing underwear.

I was wearing Tasha underwear, sexy but very beautiful underwear. I wouldn't mind people seeing it.

Person, I corrected. I wouldn't mind a person seeing it. And that person was Jamie.

Oh, boy.

He kicked off his shoes, pulled off his socks and stripped down to a pair of black boxers.

This was Jamie all right. It was all Jamie. There wasn't an ounce of James left in this man.

My hands twitched with an urge to reach out and touch him.

But he started for the pond.

I had a ridiculous desire to call Brooklyn and ask her what on earth she thought she was doing. If Jamie had been waiting to marry me in the nave of St. Fidelis, I'd have been sprinting down the aisle, desperate to get going on the honeymoon.

"Come on, Tasha," he called over his shoulder. "Live a little."

I was living.

In this moment, I felt like I was *really* living.

I pulled my T-shirt over my head. I kicked off my runners, peeled off my sweaty socks and stepped out of my pants.

The pebbles were warm on my feet. They shifted as I walked to the shore.

Jamie dived under, resurfacing with a whoop that echoed off the cliff walls. He sent ripples across the surface of the pond.

"Cold?" I asked.

"Refreshing." He swiped his hand across his wet hair as he turned to look at me. He went still then, scanning me from my head to my toes.

I was acutely conscious of my burgundy bra and panties set. It covered everything that needed to be covered. But it covered it all in sexy, stylish satin and lace.

Jamie was definitely all Jamie today. And I was sure all Tasha underneath my climbing clothes.

I waded determinedly into the water, ignoring the cold, acutely conscious of Jamie watching me.

"Refreshing," I said as the water hit my shoulders.

Goose bumps came up on my skin.

He cleared his throat. "You'll get used to it in a second."

"I think you oversold the experience," I said.

He grinned. "Wimp."

"Hey, I just climbed a rock face."

"Want to climb another?" He looked meaningfully above us.

"Dressed like this? Without equipment? I don't think so."

"Live a little," he whispered.

"This *is* living a little."

In fact, it was living a lot. I was leading a hugely exciting Tasha life here. A month ago, I couldn't have even imagined a Saturday like this.

"Up there," he said, pointing to a flat ledge about ten feet in the air. "I'm going to jump."

"Have fun."

"Come, too?"

"Scramble up that little goat track in bare feet just to jump off a rock?" I winced.

"Tasha..." he said, in the most cajoling tone I'd ever heard. He moved closer to me. "I know deep down inside your little heart is a wild woman trying to get out."

I looked around us. "This isn't wild enough?"

I was swimming in my underwear in early October.

"Not wild enough for the two of us." He waggled his brow. "It's not going to kill you."

I looked up at the ledge.

He was right. Jumping ten feet wasn't going to kill me.

I wasn't scared. And it would probably be fun. I honestly didn't know why I was so reluctant. Reflex, I supposed. Nat was used to saying no to anything that seemed weird or offbeat, anything she knew she didn't know how to do, anything that seemed frivolous or silly or without purpose.

Jumping off a rock ledge into a mountain pond was arguably silly and without purpose. But it was also arguably fun.

"Fine," I said.

Jamie looked surprised. Then he grinned. "Come on, Crazy Tasha." He started paddling to the edge of the pond.

"First I'm not wild enough, now I'm crazy? There's no pleasing you." But I followed him.

"I'm crazy, too," he called back. "In a good way."

He hoisted himself onto a space at the bottom of the rock face.

He stood and turned, offering his hand to me.

"There's a foothold about two feet under the water," he said.

I reached for his hand and found the foothold with my right foot.

His grip was strong around my hand. "Ready?"

I nodded.

Jamie hoisted. I pushed with my left. I pulled up with my free hand on the ledge, and in seconds I was out of the water standing beside him.

Our wet bodies brushed together.

I felt the glow of the contact right through to my bones.

Our gazes hit each other. They held for a sizzling moment. But then Jamie looked away, up the side of the rock, finding a path.

He marched away from me, then scrambled to the top.

"It's easy," he called back.

It looked easy. And he was right. It was easy.

In minutes we stood on the edge of the face looking down at the deep, blue-green water.

"Are you scared?" he asked.

"Not really." I might be a little nervous. Or maybe I was excited. Or maybe I was so fixated on the beauty of the man standing beside me, that I didn't really care about the long plunge into the water.

"By the way, did I tell you the latest on our stock account?" he asked.

"What happened?" I couldn't tell if it was good news or bad.

"September Innovations posted their R & D results."

"Good?" I asked cautiously.

We could stand to lose some money at this point. We could easily stand to lose some money. I knew Jamie hadn't dumped our entire portfolio into September Innovations, a wireless technology company. But he had made a substantive gamble on them.

"Come Monday morning, we'll be able to watch the graph go up and up. You should think about buying a condo."

The suggestion took me by surprise. "We just redecorated my apartment."

"You've built up a serious down payment," he said. "You should start setting up some equity now."

It was probably good advice. But my brain didn't want to delve into equity and interest rates at the moment. I'd think about it later, when I was alone, when a half-naked Jamie wasn't crowding out all the logic inside my head.

"I'll think about it," I managed between processing the images of his rugged face, his sexy body and his clinging boxers.

"Good." He reached for my hand and squeezed it in his.

I loved the strength of his grip. His energy flowed up my arm and into my chest, and nothing else in the world mattered, not one little bit.

He nodded to the pond. "On three?"

I was thinking on ten, or maybe twenty, or maybe thirty. Or maybe we could just stand here in the sunshine forever holding hands on this perfect wild and wonderful Saturday afternoon. I didn't think life could get any better.

"On three," I said.

Jamie counted. "One…"

I joined him, and together we said. "Two…three."

We jumped.

I squeezed his hand tight as we flew through the air.

It felt like a long time, but it was only seconds before my feet hit the water, then my hips, my hands, and my head went under.

Cold engulfed my senses, and I lost hold of Jamie's hand.

I bobbed down a few feet, and then buoyancy took over, pushing me back up.

I broke the surface and blinked the water from my eyes to see Jamie grinning beside me.

"I like you, Tasha," he said, his warm gaze holding mine.

"I like you too, Jamie." I meant it in ways he couldn't possibly understand.

I bicycled my feet to stay afloat in the deep water, veering toward the shore.

He kicked toward me.

His expression sobered.

He touched my shoulder, and my whole body lit with desire.

"You are beautiful," he said.

I didn't know what to say to that.

The way he was looking at me made me feel beautiful.

He feathered his hand from my shoulder to the middle of my back.

His other arm went around my waist, anchoring me, and I realized he was standing on the bottom.

I stopped moving my legs.

"Tasha," he said.

"Jamie," I answered.

He tipped his head and slowly leaned in.

His lips touched mine, cool from the water. But they heated quickly.

His kiss sent waves of wanting through my arms, my legs, to my belly and breasts. My body tightened and quickened. Passion amped up as our kiss deepened.

I wrapped my arms around him, sliding them from his firm shoulders across his back, up to his neck. My fingers tangled in the base of his hairline as I held him to me.

My lips parted farther and his tongue touched mine.

Fireworks flashed behind my eyes. Under the water, my legs wrapped around him.

Somewhere deep in my brain stem, I understood what I was doing, the intimacy of the move, what I was signaling. But my conscious mind didn't care about that.

I wanted to get closer to Jamie. I needed to get closer to Jamie. Every inch of space between us should be erased and eradicated.

His hand closed over my breast, the wet fabric making no barrier at all. I moaned with the pleasure of his touch.

I tipped my head back to give him access.

His kissed his way along my neck.

I knew where this was going. I loved where this was going. I couldn't wait to get there.

He cupped my behind, holding me to him, pressing against me, spreading pulses of heat and power in all directions.

Then he quit the kiss and gave a chopped exclamation. "We can't."

He pulled back from me. "Tasha." He took a couple of deep breaths. "I don't—"

"It's fine," I managed. I was as mortified as I'd ever been in my life. "It's nothing."

"It's not—"

"You said it yourself." I disentangled my arms and legs and put some space between us. "I'm completely refreshed."

"Tasha, wait."

"Let's get back to the car." My feet found the bottom of the pond, so I was able to propel myself even faster toward the pebble shore.

"That's not what I meant," he called from behind me. "Tasha, stop."

I wasn't stopping. The last thing I was doing was stopping.

I'd made a colossal mistake. We'd both made a colossal mistake. There was still time to correct it, and that was good.

We'd gotten over the kiss. We'd get over this.

I felt his hand on my arm.

I tried to shake it off, but he refused to let go.

He turned me, and I nearly stumbled over in the waist-high water.

"I only meant—"

"Will you let me go?" I demanded.

Maybe his precious Tasha didn't care about dignity, but Nat still did. There was still enough Nat in me to want to get the heck out of this situation.

"I don't have anything." He stared meaningfully at me, moving close up. "I don't have a condom, Tasha. I wasn't saying we shouldn't, I was saying we couldn't, not here, not now, not without protection."

His words dropped to silence.

It was a very uncomfortable silence.

"Oh." My voice was tiny. I swallowed.

He raked a hand through his hair. "What is with you?"

I didn't have a ready answer for that.

He kept talking. "Do you think I behave like that when I *don't* want to make love?"

I found my voice again. "I don't know. I couldn't tell."

"Well, *tell* already. That's what raw, unbridled lust and passion look like. You're hot, Tasha. Any guy within fifty yards of you probably wants you. And none of them, definitely not me, is going to shut it down without a damn good reason."

"Oh," I said again, struggling to shift the emotional gears inside my head.

"We should go," he said.

"Okay." I had no idea where this left us.

He moved closer. His expression changed. And my uncertainty dropped a notch.

"To your place," he said with meaning. "As fast as we can get there."

I opened my apartment door to find Sophie inside.

We both stared at each other in shock, me on finding her in my apartment—which was not unheard of, but pretty unusual—and her likely wondering why my hair was wet and why Jamie was with me.

What on earth was I going to say about that?

"Oh, good," she said before I could form any kind of a coherent sentence. "You brought Jamie. I guess you heard?" Her eyes were alight with joy.

"Uh…"

"Aaron called. Bryce and Ethan are on their way over. I can't believe it." She started to pace. "I just can't believe it. How long have you two known?"

I looked at Jamie.

We must have had identical expressions of bafflement.

"I wish you'd told me yourself," Sophie said to me. She closed the space and wrapped me in a tight hug.

Then she seemed to notice my wet hair.

She looked at Jamie, then back at me. I could see it all unraveling right here in front of us.

"Were you at the club?" she asked us.

"Yes," Jamie said.

Sophie took a step back and put her hand on her forehead. She grinned and turned away. "We need champagne."

I gave Jamie a panicked look and mouthed the word *what?*

He shrugged his shoulders.

"When Aaron told me it was five hundred thousand, I made him say it again. I couldn't believe it."

Five hundred thousand? Dollars? Did she mean *dollars*?

She turned back. "We need champagne."

"Aaron talked to you about five hundred thousand dollars?" Jamie asked.

His tone was tense, his expression worried.

"Did I get the number wrong? Oh, I hope I didn't get it wrong because I told Bryce and Ethan. Did you talk to Horatio Simms?" Her question was directed at Jamie. "Did he say that was his investment? Oh, I sure hope I didn't mess up."

"Horatio Simms is investing five hundred thousand dollars in Sweet Tech?" Jamie asked.

"I know I have you to thank for that. I don't know what you did, but—"

"I didn't talk to Horatio," Jamie said.

Sophie looked confused.

"But Aaron told me…"

"I did talk to Aaron," Jamie said. I could hear the annoyance in his voice. "Aaron must have talked to Horatio."

Sophie breathed a sigh of relief. "Oh, then that makes sense."

Jamie went to his phone.

I didn't know what was happening, but I could tell we had a big problem. There was a knock on the door.

"That'll be Bryce and Ethan." Sophie brushed past me.

"Simms?" Jamie said into the phone. "I'm at Tasha's with Sophie and her crew."

I glanced to Sophie to see if she'd noticed Jamie calling me Tasha.

She hadn't.

"When you get this," Jamie said. "Call me. Or better still, get your butt over here and tell me *what is going on*."

Jamie disconnected.

"What?" I whispered to him.

Jamie came close to my ear. "I specifically told Aaron that Sweet Tech wasn't ready for investment. It's way too high risk and we don't have a proper prospectus. I waved him off, and he pulled in his uncle instead? This is going to go *so* bad."

I didn't know what to say. I was awash with both guilt and worry. I hated the thought that I'd caused problems at work for Jamie.

"Bryce brought champagne!" Sophie said. "Get some glasses, Nat."

I forced a smile on my face. "Sure." I didn't know what else to do, so I started for the kitchen. "Can you tell me more about the deal?"

Maybe, at the very least, I could arm Jamie with some information before he talked to Aaron.

I found my champagne flutes in a high cupboard, and I passed them around.

Jamie tried to refuse, but I gave him a glare that told him to play along. There was no point in getting angry right now.

Sophie and her friends were oblivious to any problems. To them, Jamie was the hero who'd saved their fledgling business. All she could see was a bright and beautiful future of success and riches.

If it had to come crashing down, it had to come crashing down. But we should figure out exactly why before we gave her the bad news.

"To success," Sophie said, raising her glass. "And to James for all of his help."

For a second I thought Jamie might blurt something out. But he didn't, just took a drink of his champagne.

Sophie, Bryce and Ethan all started talking, fast and with plenty of emotion and excitement. I heard them say *scale up* and *distribution* and *markets*.

Before I could take Jamie aside again, there was another knock on the door.

I opened it to find Aaron.

He was grinning. "Hi, Natasha."

I could feel Jamie's presence right behind me. "Start talking, Simms."

"You heard."

"Of course I heard. Why, *why* would you tell Horatio about Sweet Tech?"

"Because I knew you were holding out on us, keeping it all to yourself."

Jamie shook his head. "That wasn't it. You knew that wasn't what was going on."

Aaron shot back, "No. I know that you told me it wasn't ready for investment."

"It wasn't. It isn't. And Horatio should know that. This isn't his kind of deal. How did you convince him to invest so much money?"

Aaron didn't answer.

"How?" Jamie repeated.

"I told him it was your recommendation."

"You *what*?" Jamie bellowed.

"I'm not an idiot, Gillen. You were going to invest. You might have wanted to dot the *i*'s and cross the *t*'s, but you know you were going to invest."

"I was *not* going to invest."

"Then why spend all that time, effort and energy on it?"

"I was doing a favor for a friend."

Aaron looked at me. "A *friend*."

His inference was clear.

"You've set your uncle up to lose money. And he's going to think I suggested it. You overconfident, cavalier little jerk."

"Nat?" Sophie's voice sounded shaky behind us.

My heart sank.

"What's going on?" Sophie asked.

There was a brittle silence. Finally, Jamie turned.

"Aaron made a mistake," Jamie said to Sophie.

"There's no mistake," Ethan said. "We have a hand-shake deal for five hundred thousand dollars."

Jamie shot Aaron a brief glare. "I need to talk to Hora-tio. He didn't have all the facts when he made that deal."

"You don't have faith in us?" Sophie asked Jamie.

Jamie didn't answer.

"It's not that," I said, trying to help.

"Tasha, don't," Jamie said.

Sophie gave him a puzzled look at the name Tasha.

"You're right," Jamie said to Sophie in a clipped, pro-fessional voice. "I don't have faith in you. The reason I don't have faith is that I'm a realist. You're at a very early stage. You need patient capital. Horatio is looking for a faster return on his investment. You're not going to be able to give it to him."

Ethan took a step forward. "Who says?"

"I say... Ethan, is it?"

"Ethan Tumble. I'm the technical brains behind this, and I know a good idea when I see one. This thing's got legs."

"I'm not saying it's not a good idea."

"We should close the door," I said.

I didn't have a lot of neighbors, but I didn't think this was a conversation we wanted people to overhear.

Jamie looked frustrated, but he stepped aside and Aaron came in.

I closed the door.

Jamie spoke again. "You may have the best idea in the world. Over the long term, you might all be headed for stellar success. And I hope you are. I really do. But it was presented to Horatio in a ridiculously irresponsible way. Aaron has to answer for that. And I have to answer for Aaron. And I will. *We* will. We'll tell Horatio the truth and take it from there."

"We're not getting the money," Sophie said, sounding completely dejected.

I didn't blame her, and I hated that I'd had a hand in setting up this debacle.

"Simms," Jamie said as he reopened the door. He gestured for Aaron to leave.

Aaron left, and Jamie followed him out.

Sophie looked like she might cry, and I realized Jamie had left me alone.

I mean, Sophie, Bryce and Ethan were still there. But Jamie was gone.

I'd come home from the hike with such high expectations for Jamie and me. This wasn't how the day was supposed to go.

The day was supposed to end with the two of us alone, together, in my bed with a condom and our pent-up passion for each other.

Ten

I wished I could have done a better job consoling Sophie. But I was fumbling in the dark. I had no idea what was going to happen next.

We speculated on the potential for Horatio's investment, and we talked about other investments that might replace it. I reminded her that she still had a good job. I told her she was young, just starting out. Things were going to go up, and things were going to go down. And I truly believed that.

Trouble was, she'd gotten her hopes way up. I knew it was hard to go from the top of the world to the depth of disappointment. It really sucked.

Privately, I wondered what Jamie and Aaron were going to say to Horatio—Aaron in favor of the investment and Jamie opposed was the best I could guess. And I really couldn't see how Horatio would be willing to invest in Sweet Tech by the end of that conversation.

A handshake deal was all well and good, but I doubted it would stand up in court. I honestly couldn't imagine Sophie suing anyone anyway.

She left at about ten thirty, after a couple of glasses of wine. We didn't have the heart to finish the champagne.

I showered the dried pond water out of my hair, using extra conditioner to get the softness back into it. Then I changed into the worn cotton shorts and T-shirt I usually wore to bed.

But I wasn't tired. I wasn't hungry. I didn't feel like watching a movie or reading a book. I wasn't even thirsty.

I prowled the apartment for a few minutes before I decided to surf around online.

I thought back on what Jamie had said about me buying a condo. I was feeling like I should get my life in order. This windfall from our investments might or might not last. I should put it to good use while I had the chance.

I'd be thirty in a couple of years. I should own my own real estate by then. That's what people did when they became full-fledged adults. They invested. They settled down. They started to build their lives.

I looked around my apartment and thought about moving. I really liked the work we'd done, the colors and the style. But it wasn't mine. It was a temporary stop for me. I considered how I could duplicate the colors and style if I bought my own condo.

Maybe I could get something on a ground floor. It would be nice not to have to lug groceries up the stairs every week. Not that it wasn't good exercise. It was very good exercise. But if I could find a place near the park, I could keep my bike handy and get exercise that way. Riding through the park would be more fun than lugging groceries up the stairs.

There was a knock on the door.

I got up to answer, my first thought being that Sophie was back. Like me, she was probably feeling way too blue to sleep. I hoped she hadn't driven her car after we'd had the wine.

Then I hesitated before opening the door.

It was really late, well after eleven. And why hadn't she texted me? She would have texted me if she was coming back.

I glanced to the dead bolt to make sure it was locked.

"Hello?" I said through the door.

"It's Jamie."

At the sound of his voice, my chest tightened with anticipation. I was glad that he'd come back, way too glad.

I quickly unlocked and opened the door.

"What happened?" I asked him, drinking in his handsome face but forcing my thoughts to Sophie. "Is it bad? Is it good? Have you talked to Sophie yet?"

He came inside. "I haven't talked to Sophie. It's too late to call her."

He was right about that. And bad news could always wait until morning. If Sophie was already asleep, it seemed cruel to wake her up only to make her more miserable.

"What happened?" I asked, hesitant to know, but knowing that not knowing wouldn't change a thing. I knew that much.

"Aaron and I talked to Horatio."

"And?" I backed away a little and braced myself.

I was pretty sure the outcome was inevitable. But once I heard the words, there was no more hope for Sophie. I felt terrible for being a part of boosting then dashing her dreams.

"It turned out badly for me," Jamie said, looking grim.

It wasn't the answer I'd expected. "I don't understand." I struggled to figure out what it might mean. "Oh, Jamie, what did Horatio do? Did you get fired"

"No. It wasn't that."

I felt a small measure of relief.

"But he won't walk away from the investment."

It took me a second to have the words make sense inside my head.

Jamie's expression was at odds with his words.

"But that's good," I said. "That means Sophie will get the money."

"No, that's bad. Yes, they'll get the money. And if they lose it, Aaron and I will be in big trouble."

I was confused. "You told Horatio the whole story, right? He knows you think it's risky. If he decided to stay in anyway—"

"Sure, I told him the whole story. Problem was, he didn't believe me."

I lowered myself into an armchair. "Why didn't he believe you?"

"He thinks I want the investment for myself."

"He thinks you'd lie to him?"

"Horatio is not exactly the trusting type. Aaron had him convinced he'd beaten me to the punch. He thinks the minute he pulls out, I'll jump in."

"Would you?" Even as I asked the question, it sounded silly.

Jamie didn't have five hundred thousand dollars to risk. And why would he put his money where it would be locked up for a long time, and where he thought he might lose it?

Why would anyone do that?

They wouldn't.

"It's still a risky investment," he said. "And if it goes bad on him, Horatio will save his reputation by putting the blame on us."

"I'm so sorry." I stood again. I was feeling worse by the minute.

"I hope I can help them. They need to get out of R & D, bring it to market and scale up."

"I'm sure you can," I said. Everything I'd seen Jamie touch had turned out well.

"Even if I can think of something, Ethan doesn't seem like the kind of guy to listen."

"You're a lot smarter than Ethan. And Sophie will listen to you."

Jamie gave a cool smile at that. "I appreciate the vote of confidence."

I didn't think Jamie needed me to tell him what he already knew. He was amazing, in so many ways. I thought it had to be obvious to the world.

We gazed at each other in silence.

Memories of our swim bloomed to life in my brain.

I wondered if he was remembering, too. I didn't know how to ask. I didn't know how to bring up the subject— the fact that I was sitting here wishing I could throw myself into his arms and pick up where we left off.

I didn't have any experience with this.

How did people tell a friend they wanted to sleep with them?

I was pretty sure they did it all the time. Friends with benefits was a thing. It was a big thing. People seemed quite taken with the concept.

It seemed like the kind of concept Tasha would like. Tasha would definitely like an arrangement like that— all the benefits and a friendship, too. Why wouldn't she want that?

And she'd ask. She'd just outright ask: *Hey, Jamie, how about we sleep together tonight?*

I snickered at myself.

"What's funny?" Jamie asked.

"Me," I said. "Tasha me."

His gaze went soft as he studied my face. "You are Tasha."

"Sometimes," I said.

I'd been very Tasha this afternoon when I jumped off that rock, then nearly jumped Jamie's bones. That had been very Tasha.

"Why is Tasha smiling?" he asked. "I'm assuming she's not amused by my predicament."

"Not at all. I'm really sorry about that."

He waved my words away. "Let's get back to the smile."

I stepped forward, bringing myself closer. It felt easier to say the words when there was some intimacy between us.

"You remember this afternoon?" I asked.

He moved too, closing the distance between us. "Is that a joke?"

"It's an opening line."

"Yes, I remember this afternoon."

I gathered every ounce of my courage and dived into the deep end. "Do you want to sleep with me?"

"Did I not make that obvious?"

"Because I want to sleep with you. There, I said it." I paused. "Okay, you probably already knew that." I recalibrated in my brain. "I'm thinking Tasha would just say it out loud. And so would Jamie. You know that Jamie would say it. If Tasha and Jamie wanted to be friends with benefits, they'd say so. They'd say it. They'd own it. They'd do it. And they'd enjoy it. No big thing. No big deal. They wouldn't dwell on whether or not it was a good idea. They're exciting. They're risk takers. They embrace life and enjoy every single moment of it. And there's no reason, none at all, why we shouldn't do exactly that. I have condoms, you know."

Jamie cracked a sudden smile. "Are you done?"

I took a breath.

Part of me couldn't believe I'd just blurted all that out.

Another part of me was darn proud for having done it. "I think so...yeah... I think that about does it."

"Yes," Jamie said.

I waited for more.

He didn't say anything else.

"That's it?" I asked.

"That's it. A solid, definitive, exciting, risk-taking yes."

I reached for his shirt.

He reached for mine.

We all but tore off each other's clothes.

Then we stopped. We stared at each other. We were mostly naked, both breathing deeply.

"I want to do this fast," Jamie said.

I was fine with fast. I was more than fine with fast. We had two perfectly good sofas within a few feet of where we were standing. And there were the armchairs. I'd make love on an armchair.

Or the floor. I'd happily make love with Jamie on the floor, too.

"But I want it to go slow." He reached out and feathered a touch on the tip of my bare shoulder.

Oh, yeah. Slow sounded marvelous.

His palm cupped my shoulder, and he drew me into a kiss.

It was long and deep and sexy sweet.

I stepped into him, my nipples brushing his chest. Tendrils of passion were winding through me, heating me straight to my core.

I wrapped my arms around his neck, leaning into the strength of him.

He cupped my rear with both hands, pulling me against him.

"But I can't do slow," he growled against my lip.

"Okay," I said.

"Slow later," he said and scooped me into his arms.

I didn't know where we were going, and I sure didn't care.

He rounded the divider in less than five seconds. Deposited me on the bed and followed me down, covering my body with his heat.

He kept up his kisses, and I molded my lips to his, thinking that he tasted good, really good, extraordinarily good. I didn't think a man's lips could taste so sweet.

His palm stroked its way up my side, over my ribs, onto my breast, settling there.

I arched my back, and a moan vibrated my lips.

His fingers wrapped my nipple, and the tingle told me it was beading in response.

"Tasha," he whispered, then stroked his tongue against mine.

I loved my name on his lips, my special, secret name that meant everything I was doing was okay. It was better than okay. It was fantastic and fun, and there wasn't a reason in the world I shouldn't be enjoying sex with Jamie.

We'd made a deal. And it was a good deal. It was a marvelous deal, and all I had to do was lie back and enjoy it.

I parted my legs to cradle him, and I stroked my hands down the length of his back, feeling the satin of his skin, the definition of his muscle, marveling at the texture and the masculine contours of his body.

I broke from his mouth to kiss his shoulder. I wanted to see if his skin tasted as good as his lips.

It did.

I kissed my way across his chest.

He threw his head back and groaned.

His fingers tightened on my nipple, sending quivers

of desire rocketing down my body. I arched into him, my legs going around his waist.

"Condom," he whispered.

Good call. For a second I'd forgotten.

I would have remembered, I told myself as I reached out and pulled open the drawer of my bedside table.

The interruption was brief, and I watched his expression until he was done and met my eyes. His were dark blue, deep and intent.

"You're gorgeous," I said.

He smiled. "You're the gorgeous one." His arms slid back around me, and he held me so tenderly close that I felt a random tear slip from the corner of my eye.

I wasn't crying. I wasn't sad. I was very, very far from sad. If anything, I wanted to whoop with joy.

"You ready?" he asked.

I'd been ready for quite a few days now.

"Yes," I said and angled toward him.

He pressed into me.

I closed my eyes, savoring every inch and every second, until we were together and desire was rocketing through my body.

He pulled, and I gasped.

His voice was a groan again near my ear. "This is *so* not going to be slow."

"Good," I said.

Slow could come later. At least, I hoped slow would come later. If making love with Jamie felt like this all the time, I didn't know how we'd ever stop.

His body met mine, and I synced our rhythm. His hands were everywhere, plucking my passion, drawing out sensations I hadn't known existed.

A colored haze took over my brain, green then blue then yellow and orange. We flew high and crested fast.

I cried out. I dived into the sun. Waves of pure ecstasy all but lifted me from the bed.

Jamie groaned, and our bodies pulsed together for long minutes.

Then I felt the tension drain from him. I melted into every touch, every sensation. My skin was slick against his. The air finally felt cool on my limbs.

"Wow," Jamie said.

"Wow," I said back.

"That was fantastic."

"It was," I agreed wholeheartedly.

"We have to do that again."

I smiled at that. I loved the conviction in his voice. "Right this second?"

"Tonight. Definitely again tonight."

His words made me think about tomorrow.

But I wasn't going to think about tomorrow. I was Tasha, and I was daring and confident, and I was going to take this moment, this night for what it was. A supergood time with a man who was becoming a supergood friend. There was absolutely no value in worrying beyond that.

It was Sunday, and I opened my apartment door to Sophie.

I was expecting Jamie in an hour, and until I saw her standing there I'd hoped the knock meant he was early. I'd hoped he was as anxious to see me as I was to see him. Then I hoped Sophie couldn't see the disappointment on my face.

She didn't.

She looked tired and frustrated.

"It's hard trying to get rich," she said and moved past me.

She was dressed in jeans and flats. Her light brown hair was swooped up in a ponytail that looked hasty. And her sparkly T-shirt hung lose over her jeans—no half tuck, no saucy knot, no nothing. This wasn't like Sophie.

"No orders yet?" I knew they'd all been contacting potential customers.

I told myself I was sympathetic. And I reminded myself how important the success of BRT Innovations was to Sophie and everyone else, including Jamie. I reminded myself that sex with Jamie was secondary to his own career and to Sophie's future.

Still, I couldn't stop thinking about his arrival. And I couldn't help hoping Sophie would be gone by then. Most of all, I couldn't help picturing Jamie naked.

"We've been at it for *months*," she said. "We're all working doubly hard now, and Jamie is helping, but there's no interest from the market. I'm talking zero interest, Nat. And it's starting to terrify me."

I closed the door. "These things take time." I knew that had to be true.

She took a couple of steps and then turned to face me. "It would be different if we had some maybes, if people liked the idea but maybe couldn't afford Sweet Tech. If they thought they might want to buy one in the future. But nobody wants to buy one in the future. They won't even consider the possibilities."

I knew I'd be a terrible salesperson. I couldn't even imagine how demoralizing it must be to face so much rejection.

"We're moving pretty fast, spending, spending, spending," she said, looking even more worried as she said it. "Ethan's put together ten more prototypes."

"You need those for sure," I said, trying to sound optimistic but feeling as worried as Sophie looked.

She gave a nervous laugh. "You have to spend money to make money?"

"I've heard that." I didn't have much else to offer.

"We're spending Horatio's money now. And the things Aaron's said about his uncle make me feel like we're indebted to a criminal—like he'll break our legs or something if we don't pay it back."

"Nobody's breaking anyone's legs." I thought about my half of the money Jamie and I had amassed and wondered if contributing it would help.

I could wait for a condo. I could be happy in my apartment for a few more years. At least it looked great now. It wasn't ugly anymore. I had that going for me.

Another knock came on the door.

My brain and my heart rooted for it to be Jamie. I couldn't help the feelings, even though I knew they were selfish.

"Aaron was going to meet me here," Sophie said.

More disappointment for me.

As I walked to the door, I told myself to stop being so self-absorbed.

Last night with Jamie had been beyond amazing, and I couldn't wait to be alone with him again, to kiss him, make love with him, to talk, to laugh, to whatever with him. I was greedy for every second we could have together.

I was greedy. And I needed to stop. Sophie needed my support right now.

I opened the door, and it was Jamie.

My heart lifted.

"Hi, Tasha," he said, his eyes warm, his lips breaking into a smile.

"Why do you call her that?" Sophie appeared at my right shoulder.

Jamie was obviously surprised to see her.

"It's short for Natasha," he said.

"So is Nat." She looked from him to me and back again. "And what are you doing here?"

Jamie didn't answer.

I opened my mouth, hoping something logical would come out of it. No reasonable explanation was forming inside my head.

Then Aaron appeared in the hallway.

"Did Aaron call you?" Sophie asked Jamie.

"He didn't have to call me," Jamie said, brushing past the awkward moment. "We work in the same office. What's going on?"

As Jamie moved past me, he purposefully brushed his hand against mine.

My skin tingled and my heart thudded.

It had been a busy week, and I was impatient to get to the benefits part of our friendship again. I was feeling *really* impatient. Clearly, I wasn't a very good friend to Sophie.

"We have to get this under control," Aaron said as he walked in the door. "We can't keep bleeding money with nothing to show for it. We need a plan to get some orders under our belt."

Bryce and Ethan arrived behind him, and my apartment filled up with the entire gang.

"We need to open some doors," Aaron said. "Nobody is taking us seriously."

"Because Sweet Tech has no track record," Jamie said, sounding impatient. "BRT Innovations has no track record. That's been my point all along."

"An 'I told you so' isn't going to help," Aaron said.

"Even if it makes you feel like the big man," Ethan tossed in.

"Ethan," I snapped.

Aaron was right. But Jamie was right, too. And Ethan being rude wasn't going to help any of it.

Jamie's eyes were annoyed, but his voice was calm. "Who have you been targeting, and where have you gone so far?"

I was impressed with his apparent self-control. Then again, I was pretty biased when it came to Jamie. I knew he had flaws, but I was hard-pressed to see any of them. He was one incredible package of a man.

I realized we'd turned him into exactly what he'd wanted—the guy that women pointed to from across the room, the guy every woman wanted to meet. And now that we'd succeeded, I didn't want it at all.

Why hadn't I just spoken up way back then, way back when no other women were looking? Why hadn't I just said, "Hey, James, date me, let's see what happens?"

I could tell myself that Nat would never have done that. But she should have done that. I should have done that. Now I felt like our time together was ticking down.

"Suppliers," Sophie said. "We've done trade shows from LA to New York. Bryce and I have taken two weeks' vacation to focus."

I was surprised to hear that. Sophie hadn't said anything to me about using up her vacation time.

"I've been through a Rolodex of suppliers," Bryce said.

"Have you tried individual restaurants?" Jamie asked. "Who are the trendsetters?"

"They can't get a return going retail," Aaron said.

"They can prove the concept," Jamie said. "And trendsetters move things on social media."

"I've tried that approach," Bryce said. "I made appointments during my downtime in New York City. I couldn't get any takers. I'd try locally, but nobody in Seattle has a big enough national profile."

Jamie paced to the kitchen corner and then turned. "Give me your elevator pitch again?"

"Perfection," Bryce said. "Zero labor, no waste, consistency and perfection."

"Who likes perfection?" Jamie asked.

Everybody looked at each other, but nobody answered.

"High-end places," Ethan suggested.

"That's where I've been *trying*," Bryce said.

"This is getting us nowhere." Aaron frowned and dropped onto a sofa.

"Nationally," Jamie said.

I could tell by his quirk of a smile that he'd thought of something.

He kept talking. "Our focus is too narrow. What about international? Who likes perfection? The French? Food is a really big deal in Paris."

"The French are all about taste," Bryce said. "They cater to sophisticated palates. The look isn't so important."

"Italy?" Jamie asked. "Asia?"

"I see what you're thinking," Bryce said. Then he gave a chopped laugh. "Japan."

"That's good," Jamie said.

"Japan?" Aaron mocked. "Your solution is to try doing business in Japan?"

"They're technology leaders themselves," Ethan said, though he looked skeptical.

"Has a Japanese company come out with a comparable product?" Jamie asked.

Ethan looked uncomfortable. "I don't know."

"Well, find out," Jamie said. "If New York doesn't want to be a trendsetter, maybe Tokyo does."

"I don't have a single contact in Japan." Sophie looked like she was close to tears.

"I have a few," Jamie said.

I couldn't help but look at him in surprise again, and maybe in awe, and maybe with an even bigger crush than I'd had ten minutes ago.

Was there anything he couldn't do?

Jamie had his phone out and was pressing buttons.

"Ethan, you need to get a prototype packed and ready to ship with us. Bryce, keep working on individual restaurants. They may end up being our only hope. Try LA next. They must have trendsetters in LA. Sophie?"

Sophie glanced at him. "Yes?"

"Want to go to New York with me?"

"Me?" she asked, looking surprised, beautiful and surprised.

I was surprised, too. Not that I didn't trust Sophie's business acumen. I did. But Bryce was the chef and Ethan was the tech specialist.

"Rina Nanami is in New York City right now. The Nanami family is a client, and they own a chain of high-end restaurants in Japan. Our best bet is for her to meet one of the owners in person. It has to be Sophie because Rina will like that she's a woman entrepreneur. That's our ticket in through the door."

I fought a lump in my throat.

I was glad that Jamie had an idea. I was excited for Sophie and for everyone.

And I wouldn't be jealous of Sophie going to New York with Jamie. I got that she was the business owner and not me. Besides, Sophie wasn't interested in Jamie. She was with Bryce.

And, anyway, Jamie and I were just friends. I didn't have the right to be jealous of him with anyone.

But I wanted it to be me in New York, me with Jamie, me on a cross-country flight in his company.

He looked at me then.

I could tell what he was thinking. At least, I hoped I could tell what he was thinking. What I wanted him to be thinking was that he'd miss me. Better still, I wanted him to be thinking he'd stay here tonight, that he'd wait until everyone else left and then he and I could have benefits again.

I wanted him to spend the night this time. I wanted to watch the dawn break in his arms, share coffee in my little rooftop garden, laugh together over toast or eggs or blueberry bagels.

I wanted Jamie to myself.

I didn't want him to fly off with Sophie.

The countdown on our relationship felt like it was ticking louder than ever.

"It'll be a whirlwind trip," he said to me. "I'm…" After a second, he clamped his jaw, seeming to become aware that all gazes were on him.

"Good luck," I said in the brightest voice I could muster.

"I want to be there by morning," he said. "It'll give us the best chance of catching Rina."

He was talking to everyone, but his gaze was still on me.

I thought he was apologizing. At least, I hoped he was apologizing. I wanted him to be as disappointed about tonight as I was. But I couldn't be sure that was happening. It was impossible to know.

It was bad enough to be jealous of Sophie.

I'd spent two days being jealous of Sophie.

But as I walked into the O'Neil Nybecker offices, I had a whole new reason to be jealous.

I'd felt good leaving home to drive over here. Jamie was back, and he'd asked me to meet him at the office. I assumed we were going out for dinner, maybe we'd do a little downtown shopping, or maybe we'd look at houses again. Whatever it was, I'd like being back on track.

As long as we ended up back at my place later on, or maybe his place this time. Friends with benefits was way more fun when you found time for the benefits.

I'd put on a pale blue crepe dress with a flowing gray speckled sweater over top. Both hung to midthigh, leaving a length of bare leg to show off my shimmery, dusty-blue ankle boots. They weren't perfect for walking, but they were better than spike-heeled sandals or pumps. I'd topped the dress off with a chunky bright blue necklace.

I'd felt chic and funky, quite pretty, really. That is, until I spotted Sophie laughing next to Jamie in a royal blue cocktail dress. It was fitted and sleek, with a straight neckline and wide shoulder straps. Sophie looked ready for a night on the town.

Worse, on the other side of Jamie was a lovely, petite Japanese woman. She wore a short, jewel-encrusted jacket over a pleated white skirt. Her dark hair was swooped up, and her jewels looked like real diamonds. She had her hand on Jamie's arm, and he was whispering something in her ear.

They looked fantastic together, a power couple out to conquer the world.

I tried to capture the feeling I'd had when I gazed in the mirror earlier. But it was gone. The sweater that had seemed so fashion forward then felt dowdy now.

"Natasha." It was Aaron who spotted me first. "Did you hear the good news?"

I hadn't heard any news. Although Jamie had definitely sounded upbeat when he'd called and asked me to meet him at the office.

"What's going on?" I asked Aaron.

"We're about to pop the champagne."

"For?" I prompted.

"The contract, of course."

"Of course," I said.

"And all the rest," he said with a grin.

Sophie spotted me then and rushed forward. "Nat. There you are!"

I was grateful for her enthusiastic greeting, but I

couldn't help wanting Jamie to notice me, too. So far he was still absorbed in conversation with the pretty woman who still had her hand on his arm.

"Isn't it fantastic?" Sophie asked.

"I don't know what's going on," I told her.

"We got a deal. Rina Nanami, well, her family, the Nanami Corporation, have put in an order for Sweet Tech. A *big* order for their restaurant equipment distribution company in Tokyo. They have customers all over Asia, their own restaurants and a bunch of others. James is thrilled. He says Horatio is thrilled."

Aaron reappeared and handed Sophie and I each a flute of champagne.

I was a little surprised that O'Neil Nybecker would pull out the stops like this to celebrate the sale. I mean, it was fantastic for Sophie and BRT Innovations. But it couldn't be that big of a deal to O'Neil Nybecker. I mean, in the greater scheme of things.

Just then, an older man appeared from a corner office. He was quickly handed a glass of champagne, and the attention all turned to him.

"That's Horatio," Sophie whispered to me.

When I compared him to Aaron, I could see the family resemblance.

Everyone went quiet.

"Thank you all for helping us to celebrate today," he said to the assembled crowd.

I glanced around at executives of all ages in suits, skirt suits and classic dresses.

"To O'Neil Nybecker's newly expanded relationship with Nanami Corporation. Thank you to James Gillen and Rina Nanami for getting the ball rolling. We look forward to our firms' future together in technology and beyond.

Ms. Nanami, please extend my sincerest thank-you to your grandfather. We look forward to visiting Tokyo soon."

Horatio held up his glass.

Everyone followed suit and took a drink.

It took me a second to remember to take a sip.

Clearly, there was more going on here than a contract for Sweet Tech.

"Good trip?" I asked Sophie. My tone sounded darker than I'd intended.

She gave me an odd look. "Fantastic, of course."

Jamie still hadn't looked at me. Rina Nanami had all of his attention. I was wishing I'd stayed home.

"I take it James did more than the Sweet Tech contract?"

"Is something wrong?" Sophie asked.

"No. Why would anything be wrong?"

"You tell me. Are you jealous?"

I almost spilled my champagne. I couldn't believe Sophie had pegged me so fast. What had I said? How had I given away my feelings? This was mortifying.

"I'm not a millionaire yet or anything," Sophie said. There was a teasing tone to her voice. "It was a good sale, but you and I are still friends." She gave me a nudge on the arm. "And, anyway, I'll still hang out with you when I'm filthy rich."

I managed a smile. It was a smile of relief. My secret was still safe.

"I'm not jealous," I told her. "And I don't want to be filthy rich."

"I'll take us on a cruise," she said. "You and me in the South Pacific, hanging out on the beach, barefoot waiters bringing us blender drinks."

"You just used up all your vacation." I ordered myself not to look at Jamie.

"After we make the first million, I'm quitting my job."

I managed a chuckle at that. "What about Bryce? Won't he want to go on a cruise with you?"

She waved a dismissive hand. "Oh, that's not going anywhere."

"What? I thought it was a thing. He seems really nice." I couldn't help it. My thoughts went to Jamie again. Was it Sophie I needed to worry about and not Rina Nanami?

I hated myself for thinking that way.

"We decided not to mix business and a relationship," Sophie said.

"You didn't meet someone else?" I hated to ask, but I didn't want to have to wonder. Wondering would be painful.

The alternative was asking Jamie. And I didn't think I could bring myself to do that.

"*When* would I have met someone else?" she asked.

"Oh. Okay." I felt worse. No, I felt better. No, I felt stupidly selfish and suspicious. "Are you okay about it?" Remembering I was her best friend, I checked her expression for signs of heartbreak.

"I'm fine. It was a mutual decision."

"How mutual?" Like me, Sophie had bemoaned her single status after Layla and Brooklyn each got married.

"*Very* mutual. I'll be more than happy to go on a girlfriend cruise. I won't mope around."

My gaze moved to Jamie. I was afraid I might mope around without him.

He caught my eye then, and he smiled. A big, not-a-care-in-the-world smile as if he hadn't been standing there flirting with Rina Nanami and ignoring me for the past fifteen minutes.

He said something to her, maybe excusing himself, maybe telling her he'd be right back, maybe setting a time to meet up with her later…at his place…for wild and crazy sex in his king-size bed.

I knew my imagination was out of control. And I knew I was being stupid, stupid, stupid about my friend with benefits. My job was to help him become attractive to women. If the past few minutes were anything to go by, I could check that one as a success.

But I couldn't help but wonder what had happened between them in New York. They'd been together there for two whole days and seemed to have made the business deal of the year. Clearly, they respected each other. Maybe they admired each other. Obviously they liked each other, quite a lot I had to imagine.

You didn't make the business deal of the year with someone unless you liked them a lot. And Rina Nanami seemed perfect for the new Jamie. She was worldly, successful, sophisticated, exciting. Men definitely pointed at her from across the room. They'd be jealous of Jamie if she was by his side.

They might have had a whirlwind romance in New York. Maybe there'd be no more benefits for me. Maybe Jamie was now taken.

I knew I could ask Sophie if something had happened between Jamie and Rina, but I'd give myself away for sure if I started quizzing her on that.

"Hi, Tasha," he said.

He didn't hug me. He didn't kiss me. He didn't even shake my hand.

I didn't like that.

"Did Sophie tell you we're all going to dinner?"

"All of us?" I asked.

Jamie paused for a second. "Yes. All of us. It's a celebration."

"Great," I said, forcing a note of cheer into my voice. "That's great."

Sophie motioned to Bryce and Ethan.

What? Jamie mouthed to me.

"Nice trip?" I asked him.

I tried to stop myself, but my gaze went to Rina Nanami.

Jamie followed my gaze.

"Sophie told you?" he asked.

The bottom fell right out of my stomach. I was stunned for a moment. I wanted to ask him why he'd bothered inviting me here. Did he want to show off Rina Nanami? Was she proof that our little experiment worked, that our little game together was over?

"I didn't think she'd do that," he said.

"No reason not to," I said.

Sophie didn't know I was falling for Jamie. Heck, Jamie didn't know I was falling for Jamie. I was completely alone here in my heartbreak.

"It's really my news," he said.

"Okay." I waited for him to give it to me with both barrels. I told myself I'd take it well. I'd congratulate him and make an excuse to go home. Maybe I had a headache. I did have a headache. At least, I was developing a headache. I'd have one soon, I could tell.

"Head office is a huge step," he said. "Guys wait decades for an offer like the one they gave me."

I blinked at him.

I might have also cocked my head sideways in confusion.

I dropped my mouth open, hoping for logical words to come out. Nothing did.

Eleven

I sat next to Sophie at dinner.

It was an oversize round table that made it feel like we were slightly too far apart. Aaron was on the other side of Sophie, then Bryce, Jamie, Rina around to Ethan next to me.

Sophie leaned close, keeping her voice low. "Tell me again why Brooklyn didn't marry James."

The question made me look at Jamie. Looking at Jamie made me want him.

After hearing Jamie's big news was a promotion to the head office in LA, I wasn't as jealous of Rina. But it was still clear she liked him. She liked him a lot. As did both waitresses, and I thought the hostess might try to give him her number before we left.

"She met Colton," I said to Sophie, my voice equally low. "She fell in love with Colton."

"I suppose," Sophie said. "But why she'd go looking, I'll never understand."

I didn't want to be jealous of Sophie again. I hated that feeling.

I told myself admiring Jamie was a long way from

making a serious play for him. I didn't think Sophie would do that, not given his history with Brooklyn.

I shouldn't be doing it, either.

I wasn't doing it. Not really.

I was just mooning over him, wishing I could sleep with him again and trying to keep my feelings under control. That wasn't the same as making a serious play for him.

"I don't know why she did, either," I said to Sophie.

It wasn't the first time I'd wondered about Brooklyn's decision.

If I was with Jamie, really with Jamie, not a friend, not a coconspirator on a life-improvement quest, but with him like Brooklyn had been with him, I'd never look at another man.

"Do you think he dates?" Sophie said.

I was pretty sure he didn't. At least, he'd never said anything about dates he'd had since Brooklyn. I knew he'd like to date. That was the whole point of everything we'd been doing.

I wished right then I could tell Sophie about me and Jamie. I wanted to share my confusion and fear, and the thrill I'd felt sleeping with him. Those were the kinds of things best friends shared.

"I expect he wants to move on," I said to her instead.

"I'd date him," she said.

My fork dropped from my hand.

"I mean," she continued, "if he asked, and if there was a spark, if I could stop thinking of him as a brother." She heaved a sigh. "Man, I wish I could stop thinking about him as a brother."

Relief washed over me. At least I didn't have to worry about Sophie.

I picked up my fork.

"Why do you suppose you feel that way?" I was curious. Especially since it turned out I didn't think of Jamie as a brother at all.

"I've known him since I was four, I suppose. And he's kind of always been there in the background, helping us build that playhouse, driving us to the movies, moving our stuff into the college dorms. You know, brother stuff."

I also thought it was all-around great guy stuff. But I wasn't about to start waxing poetic about him.

I caught his gaze across the table. But it only lasted for a split second. Rina was talking, and his attention went back to her.

"Does she seem like his type?" I asked Sophie.

"She's pretty," Sophie said.

"Brooklyn's pretty, too."

Both Rina and Brooklyn were ultrafeminine. I couldn't help wondering how my athletic rock climbing and practical apartment renovation pursuits came across to him. Did he think of me as feminine, or maybe sturdy…sturdy and plain? It occurred to me that, when all was said and done, Tasha might not be all that far from Nat.

"He's a great-looking guy. Great-looking guys date pretty women."

I wanted to change the subject now. "Bryce is a good-looking guy," I said in a low tone.

"Are you interested in Bryce?"

Sophie's response took me aback. I hadn't been thinking that at all. Bryce seemed nice. He seemed fine. He seemed, well, brotherly really when I thought about it. I had no romantic interest in Bryce whatsoever.

"That wasn't what I meant," I said.

"Well, you didn't warm up to Ethan."

"Are you saying I'm picky?"

Sophie grinned. "Very picky. But in a good way. You should be picky. You're wonderful."

I wished I felt wonderful. But this wasn't a wonderful-feeling kind of evening.

Jamie laughed at something Rina said. On her other side, Ethan laughed, too.

"I'm going to the ladies' room," I said to Sophie.

I felt like I needed to stretch my legs and breathe for a minute.

"Do you want dessert?" Sophie asked. "Should I order you something if the waitress asks?"

"Sure," I said. "Pick something decadent."

I'd seen a few desserts go by, destined for other tables, and they looked fantastic. I wasn't above consoling myself with sugar.

I left the table and retreated to the elegant quiet of the ladies' room. In the powder area I took my time, washing my hands, combing my hair, taking my sweater off for a minute to see if I liked the look better in just the dress. It was different, but I wouldn't say better. I should have gone with a more fitted dress, and maybe jazzier earrings. Strappy sandals wouldn't have been the worst idea, either.

When I'd dressed, I'd thought we might be going house shopping for Jamie. I'd thought I might be walking a lot. I didn't want to walk through houses in spike heels. But I could have done spike heels across a restaurant, easy.

When I decided I couldn't put it off any longer, I left the powder room, coming into the hallway back to the dining room.

Jamie suddenly appeared.

He grasped my hand and pulled me against him, stepping back into a small alcove.

He kissed me there. It was a deep, long, tender kiss that had my entire body sighing with joy.

His arms went around me, and mine went around him. I molded myself to the breadth of his chest and his sturdy thighs.

He cradled my hair and tucked my face into the crook of his shoulder.

"This isn't what I wanted," he said.

I really hoped he didn't mean the kiss.

He kept talking. "Nanami is a huge, huge account."

"I got that." I had.

There was nothing Jamie could have done to get out of this dinner. And he shouldn't have done anything. He'd made huge strides for Sweet Tech and for O'Neil Nybecker. He'd done everything right.

I felt a little guilty for sulking.

He kissed me again, and I felt nothing but wonderful.

But then we heard voices and footsteps.

We broke apart. We weren't alone in the hallway anymore.

I went one way, back to the table. And Jamie went the other toward the men's room.

"You okay?" Sophie asked as I sat back down.

"Fine," I said, assuming she was worried about how long I'd been gone.

"You look flushed."

I felt flushed. "It's a bit hot in here. Plus the glass of wine. You know."

She was still peering closely at my face.

"Did you order dessert?" I asked to change the subject.

"Raspberry chocolate mousse."

"Sounds perfect."

I watched Jamie sit back down.

The waiter put a beautifully decorated plate in front of me. But I knew the mousse wouldn't be anywhere near as sweet as Jamie's kiss.

* * *

I wished I could have left the restaurant with Jamie. But I had my car, and he had his. It made the most sense for me to drop off Sophie and Ethan. And Jamie was acting as host for Rina.

I told myself not to be jealous. Jamie's kiss in the hallway had gone a long way to making me feel desirable. It was a fantastic kiss. It showed me how much I'd missed him.

If I wanted to worry about something, I should worry about that.

He wasn't mine to miss, but my heart had started pretending he was.

I'd have to watch that. I'd have to watch it very closely. Maybe not Rina, but someday, likely someday soon, Jamie was going to meet Brooklyn's replacement, and I was going to be collateral damage when that happened.

It was good that I'd come home alone.

Good, I told myself as I came to the top of the staircase in my building. So good. "Really frickin' good," I muttered.

Something moved in the shadows of the hall.

I froze.

"I hope I wasn't too presumptuous," Jamie said, stepping into view from my doorway.

My heart nearly thumped from my chest. "You scared me half to death."

"Sorry," he said.

My fear was turning to joy, but my feet stayed plastered to the floor.

He moved toward me. "I needed to see you. It was driving me crazy, you sitting there, us not being able to talk about anything."

"It did feel like an awfully huge secret," I said.

Concern flashed across his face. "It's nobody's business."

"I know." I agreed with that. At least, conceptually, I agreed with that. But Sophie was a pretty close friend.

He framed my face with his hands. "We don't owe anyone an explanation."

"I know," I said again.

His smile was tender. "Tasha doesn't explain."

I reached for my Tasha-ness. "Tasha does whatever she wants."

He gave me a slow kiss that curled my toes.

He moved his lips half an inch from mine. "What does Tasha want to do?"

"You," I said with bald honesty.

I wrapped my arms around his neck and put my pent-up desire into a kiss.

"Oh, yeah," he whispered, wrapping me tight and propelling us to the door.

I fumbled for my key, struggling to slide it into the lock until Jamie's hand closed over mine to steady it.

"You okay?" he asked.

I nodded. "Fine."

"Nervous?"

The very last thing I felt was nervous—excited, energized, aroused. I felt all of those things.

"I'm not nervous," I said.

"Good."

The key slipped into the lock and the sound of the tumblers turning seemed to echo.

Jamie turned the knob and pushed the door open.

"I'm not nervous, either," he said as he closed it behind us.

I couldn't help but smile at that.

"What are you?" I asked.

"Happy."

"Me, too."

"I missed you," he said.

"So did I."

He smoothed back my hair and gazed into my eyes. "I missed this."

He kissed me tenderly.

A sigh coursed all the way through me.

He pushed the sweater from my shoulders and tossed it on a chair.

I did the same with his suit jacket.

"But not just this," he said between kisses. "I don't want you to think—"

"That it's all about sex?"

"It's not."

"I know. We've had sex exactly once."

"Twice," he said. "Did you forget?"

"I meant one night."

We'd definitely made love twice that night. The second had taken a long time, a really, really long and wonderful time.

"Okay," he said.

I pushed the buttons of his dress shirt through the holes, gradually revealing his bare chest.

He stood still and let me work.

I parted the two sides. I kissed his chest, tasting the salt of his skin.

He sucked in a breath.

"I really want to go slow this time," he said.

"Me, too." I pushed his shirt from his shoulders and let it drop to the floor.

"I'm not just saying that," he said.

"Neither am I."

I lifted the front of my dress and drew it over my head.

I tossed it aside and stood in my bra and panties. They were a pretty set, translucent white lace with shiny silver details.

"Don't move," he said.

I stilled.

He took a step back, and his gaze traveled from my boots to my eyes.

"My work here is most definitely done," he whispered.

Judging by the glow in his eyes, he didn't mean the sex was over, so I smiled.

He moved in and smoothed back my hair. "You are hands down the first and only woman who men will point at from across the room."

"If I'm dressed like this, they probably will."

"If you're dressed like anything."

"I think your judgment is clouded right now."

I was thrilled Jamie was so sexually attracted to me. I was absolutely attracted to him.

"Take off your pants," I said to him.

"Demanding."

"If you get to check me out, I want equal time."

"Yes, ma'am," he said.

He kicked off his shoes and stripped out of his pants and socks. He was down to his black boxers.

I pretended to consider him for a moment.

"And?" he prompted.

"I'd point," I said.

"Good to know."

"Other women would point, too."

"I think I need to flash a fancy car and a big credit card to guarantee their interest."

"Oh, no, you don't."

I came close enough to trail my fingers down his chest. "You've got pecs and a six-pack."

"Lots of guys have that."

I came closer still, setting my hands on his shoulders. "And really broad shoulders with that confident stance."

"I have been practicing."

I touched his chin, moving it to one side and then the other.

"Why do I feel like livestock at an auction?"

"Strong, square chin," I said. "You can't buy that."

"With the right plastic surgeon, you can."

"Not like yours. And your eyes…" I felt myself falling into their depths.

"What about my eyes?"

"*Best* blue eyes ever. They show off your intelligence, and they glow when you smile or when you make a joke. Women like a sense of humor."

I meant all of it. I meant everything I was saying, and the power of my emotions scared me.

"My lips?" he asked on a whisper.

I set aside my fear. "Kissable."

"That's exactly what I was going for." He kissed me. He pulled me close.

Our bodies meshed together, every bulge met with a corresponding hollow. We fit. We fit so perfectly.

His hands roamed my body, arousing every inch, igniting passion along every trail they took. He peeled off my bra and cupped my breasts, sending tiny shock waves through my core, making my limbs twitch in anticipation.

He stripped off my panties and then his boxers.

He lifted me to perch on the back of the sofa, easing between my thighs.

"Condom," I said.

"Got it."

I hugged him close, surrounded him, absorbed his kisses, took his caresses and gave back with my own.

Our bodies were slick as we moved together.

I was hot. His skin was hotter.

His scent surrounded me. His kisses enveloped me. His caresses made me gasp with pent-up desire and burning anticipation.

"Now," I finally groaned, completely out of patience.

"Slow," he said, but his hand kneaded hard on my lower back.

"Too slow."

"Okay." He shifted me. He moved. He eased inside.

I felt the world stop. Every molecule of me was focused on him.

He pressed deep, and I spiraled upward. Again and again and again, until I lost track of time and space.

I kissed him over and over. I clung to his shoulders, ran my hands down his back, pulled him against me and into me, climbing to the top and then finding more.

When I hit the edge and fell, I called out his name.

"Tasha," he groaned. "Tasha, Tasha, Tasha."

I was limp, and he carried me to my bed, flipping back the covers and climbing inside.

We made love again. Slower this time, more sweetly, less passionately, a soft and satisfying echo.

Later, when I felt Jamie move, I realized I'd fallen asleep in his arms.

I opened my eyes to see dawn barely filtering into the sky beyond the window.

His body was warm, wrapped around mine from behind. He put a featherlight kiss on the back of my neck.

"Again?" I muttered.

That would make three.

"I wish," he said, a low chuckle in his voice.

I shifted, settling to a more comfortable position.

"Maybe," he said with a teasing lilt.

"Optimist."

He was quiet for a moment, his breath caressing the hairline at the back of my neck.

I savored the feeling, clung to the moment. I wanted to stop time and never leave this place.

"You should come with me," he said, his voice a low rumble.

My first thought was no. I didn't want either of us to move, ever, not even an inch.

"Where are you going?" I asked after a minute.

He rose onto his elbow and rolled me so he could look at my face. "Los Angeles, remember?"

I did.

He'd been offered a job in O'Neil Nybecker's head office. Their head office was in Los Angeles. I knew that. It just hadn't been foremost in my mind.

Right now, I thought he'd meant breakfast. But he didn't. Jamie was leaving Seattle.

"Come," he said, an eager light in his eyes.

The single-word invitation swirled through my brain, hitting synapses, gathering data, analyzing and comparing to known information, seeking meaning.

I was afraid to hope. But my blooming heart colored my thoughts.

Was he saying…?

Could he possibly be suggesting…?

Did I dare hope he was asking for something more than friendship, something romantic? Was it possible that of all the adoring women in the world, Jamie might be interested in me?

My head was nodding before I thought it all through.

His grin went wide. "Great. We can carry right on with the house hunting."

I hesitated. Wait. What?

"I want a wild and exciting Tasha-and-Jamie type house."

A house? He wanted me to help him find real estate? Like any good friend would do? I would have laughed if it didn't hurt so much.

"You up for that?" he asked.

"Sure," I said, trying desperately to match his smile. Then I eased away from him.

His arm went quickly around my stomach. "Where are you going?"

"It's almost morning." Cuddling with my friend-with-benefits had suddenly lost its appeal.

"What time do you usually get up?"

"It takes me a while to shower," I said.

He kissed me again.

I kissed him back, and it felt good. But it was a bitter-sweet good. Last night we'd reached the pinnacle, and there was nowhere to go but down.

I didn't want to give up our friendship. But I knew it would never be the same.

And that was my fault.

It was all my fault.

Jamie had stuck to the rules of the game. I was the one who had broken them.

On the plane to Los Angeles, Jamie showed me our latest stock portfolio numbers.

I was surprised to find we were flying first-class. Not that I didn't like it. I liked it a lot. But it seemed like an extravagant waste of money.

So he'd pulled out his phone.

I'd stared at the numbers, thinking there had to be a mistake.

He'd laughed at my astonishment. Then he'd teased me about having too little faith in Jamie's instincts for trading.

Then he'd given me a half hug and told me he'd booked a five-star hotel.

So here we were at the Chatham-Brix Downtown, checked into a suite with a sweeping view of the city.

I had mixed feelings about sleeping with Jamie again.

Oh, I wanted to sleep with Jamie again. No matter what else was going on in our relationship, the sex was off the charts. And I hadn't had a lot of off-the-charts sex in my life. I'd really never had much at all.

I'd certainly never had any that came close to Jamie.

But the friends thing was hard. I was lying now when I called us friends. My feelings for him had gone way beyond friendship. And when the sex stopped, when everything stopped, as it would as soon as he moved to LA, it was going to hurt so much.

I'd done heartbreak once, and I had no desire to do it again.

I told myself Tasha could handle it better than Nat. But myself didn't really believe it. It was going to be even worse this time because what I'd felt for Henry was nothing, nothing compared to what I felt for Jamie.

"Marnie arranged all three viewings for this afternoon," Jamie said, coming in from the wraparound balcony. "Traffic looks busy, so we better get going."

I knew the houses we were going to see. I'd helped Jamie pick them out on the real estate website before we'd left Seattle. They were all in Santa Monica. One was even on the beach.

We ended up going to the beach home first. It was a sleek modern condo on the ground floor with a patio walkway to the lush green lawn across the road from a sandy beach. It had a lot of white walls, glass features and stark marble countertops, both in the kitchen and bathrooms.

The master bedroom had a gas fireplace, which I loved. And the patio had a fun wraparound sofa and gas fire pit. I could see it would be cozy on cool evenings. But the neighbors were pretty close, as was the traffic noise.

When we saw the second house, I thought I understood the real estate agent Marnie's strategy. Away from the beach, you could get a whole lot more for your money.

The second house was bigger. It was private, with a big yard and hedges that screened the neighbors. There was a pool and patio out back, and beautiful landscaping in the front. It was also on a quiet street.

It had a white interior with lots of archways and some wrought-iron features. The floors were beautiful hardwood with scattered area rugs. Paned doors and windows into the backyard let in enormous amounts of light. And the kitchen was a dream, tons of counter space, cupboard space, and glass-fronted feature cabinets. An octagonal breakfast nook stuck out into the backyard. I could picture Jamie having coffee there in the morning.

The master bedroom was roomy and beautiful. But I couldn't bring myself to linger there. While I could picture myself in the bed with Jamie in the hotel room, here in what might be his new house, I could only picture faceless, nameless other women in his arms.

I pretended to check out the guest bedroom.

Marnie had assumed we were a couple, and Jamie hadn't corrected her. It made it worse when she talked like I'd be cooking in the kitchen or swimming in the pool, or showering in the en suite. But I tamped down my flailing emotions and played along. What else was I going to do?

The sun was setting by the time we made it to the last house. My first impression was of warm lights on the palm trees decorating the front yard. Around and above the front door were two stories of glass walls. The polished maple ceiling colored the glow from the entry hall.

The house was a roomy open concept. Walls were painted white, but the maple trim and maple flooring warmed the atmosphere. The kitchen had stainless appliances and gray speckled countertops. It opened to a big, furnished deck with a built-in fireplace, barbecue and kitchenette. You could see the ocean in the distance.

I could imagine entertaining here. I could see friends and family—Jamie's friends and family, of course—spilling out from the family room and kitchen, onto the deck on a warm summer night.

The master bedroom had a peaked maple beamed ceiling and its own private sundeck. I told myself not to linger in it, but my toes curled into the plush carpet, and I kind of fell in love with the steam shower and gloriously huge bathtub.

"What do you think?" Jamie asked, coming up behind me.

"There's a lot to like," I said.

"Values in this neighborhood have steadily climbed for the past three years," Marnie said. "There's no end in sight."

"What do you like?" Jamie asked me.

"What do *you* like?" I said instead.

He glanced around. "It's the new me."

I told myself Jamie deserved this.

Whatever came his way next, he wasn't the James who'd been left at the altar. He was confident and decisive, great looking and a very exciting man. He had a new job, soon a new house, all his new clothes and hobbies. I was sure they had rock climbing in California.

The world was his to enjoy.

I had to be happy for him.

"I think you'll love entertaining on the deck," I said.

"Do *you* love the deck?"

"I do," I said. "And the yard. There's room out there to garden and to lounge. And you can't beat that en suite." I gestured to the attached bathroom.

"Is it a buy?" he asked.

"It's pretty expensive." It was also really big for one person.

"That's the beauty of short-term trading," he said. "What was unaffordable two months ago is now completely within range."

"I have you to thank for that." I was thinking I really would go condo shopping back in Seattle. It would give me something to focus on for the next few months.

I was going to get through this.

I knew I was going to get through this.

I'd refuse to do anything else.

"We'll take it," Jamie said to Marnie.

She looked shocked, but she recovered quickly. "I can help you write up the offer. Did you have a price in mind?"

Jamie looked at me. "Should we start low?"

"Do you want to dicker?" I wasn't a fan of the negotiating process.

Maybe Tasha would like to bargain. I didn't really know. It was getting hard to tell what the Tasha me would want versus the Nat me.

"Not really," Jamie said.

"If you go twenty-five thousand below asking, I can pretty much guarantee they'll accept."

Jamie looked at me.

I shrugged my shoulders. The game was over. It was his decision, his money, his life.

"Done," he said to Marnie. "Write it up."

"Subject to financing?" she asked.

He smiled and shook his head. "No need. I'm sure I can arrange the financing."

Marnie beamed. "Then congratulations. I'm guessing you want an early closing date."

Jamie squeezed my hand. "The earlier the better. They want me to start in the LA office on Monday."

I forced myself to smile, to keep up the facade for Marnie's sake.

I wanted to cling to Jamie and never let go. At the same time, I wanted to get the heck out of LA and never look back. I knew in that second that I couldn't stay the night. I couldn't make love to Jamie one last time in that opulent hotel suite. It would kill me.

"I'll get started." Marnie dialed a number as she left the bedroom.

"This is terrific," Jamie said to me.

I pretended my phone buzzed and pulled it from my purse. "I should take this," I said.

"Sophie?" he asked.

I nodded. I don't know why I thought a silent lie was better than a verbal lie, but I did.

I moved a couple of paces away. "Hi," I said into the phone.

I waited a minute, feeling terribly, utterly awful about what I was doing.

I scrambled for a viable reason to leave.

"She did?" I said into the phone. "Uh, okay." I looked at Jamie to find him watching me. "I can. If you think so."

"What?" he mouthed.

I held up one finger, trying to stall as I solidified my plan. It was shameless. It was probably unforgivable. But I didn't have a better idea, and I was running out of time.

"As soon as I can," I said into the phone. "Bye."

"What?" Jamie asked.

"It's Brooklyn," I said. "I don't know what's going on, but Sophie wants me to come back to Seattle."

Jamie clamped his jaw.

I knew he wouldn't ask about Brooklyn. It was the one thing he'd stay miles away from.

"I'm sorry," I said.

"Don't go."

"I have to." I wanted to cry. I wanted to collapse into a puddle of guilt. But mostly, I wanted to throw myself into his arms for as long as he'd have me.

We could hear Marnie's muted voice outside the room.

"You don't need me for this part," I said.

He opened his mouth, but I kept on talking.

"I'll book a flight in the cab."

"You're going *now*? Right now?"

"I'm sorry," I said again.

"How soon can you come back?"

"I don't know."

"You'll come back as soon as you can."

I nodded, another silent lie. I'd come up with more excuses later if Jamie pushed it.

He might not push it. He probably wouldn't push it. He'd get settled here in this great new house, with his great new job, and a great new girlfriend within a week or a month, surely not longer than that.

He'd have the life he'd wanted, just like we'd planned.

"My assistant has started on the paperwork," Marnie said brightly as she came back into the master bedroom. "We can swing by the office and sign, and I'll present the offer tonight."

"Good luck," I said to Jamie. I was already calling a cab.

Twelve

Five days, thirty texts and seven missed phone calls later, I decided I had to bring Sophie in on my deception. Jamie was more persistent than I'd expected, and I was afraid he might reach out to Sophie. If he did, he'd discover my lie.

I didn't want him to know I'd lied. For some reason, that was important to me.

I poured Sophie and me each a glass of merlot.

"We got another big order today," Sophie was saying.

She'd kicked off her shoes and curled up on one end of my sofa.

"Congratulations." I thought about recorking the bottle, but I had a feeling we'd finish it off before the evening was done.

"Japan was for sure the place to go. Cash is starting to flow in, and we've gone into actual production. Ethan's looking at expanding the facility to the space next door."

"I'm so glad it's working out." I really was.

Sophie's success was a bright spot in my dismal-feeling life.

"I'm not ready to quit The Blue Fern yet. Neither is Bryce. But we're talking about approaching the general manager with a proposal to job share. We'd each work half-time, and hire another person to take up the slack. That way, we don't need to take a full salary from BRT, but we'll have more time to devote to building up the company."

"That sounds like a good idea." I wished I could focus on Sophie's company, but I was painfully distracted.

I handed her one of the glasses and took the other end of the sofa.

My shoes were already off, and I turned sideways to face her, leaning my back against the arm.

"What about you?" she asked.

"What about me?" I told myself to take the opening and plunge right in, but I didn't know how to start.

"What's going on?" She took a sip. "Oooh. That's good."

"It's not too expensive," I said, taking a drink myself. Inwardly I was kicking myself for being a coward. I had to speak up already.

"I did something," I said.

Sophie's brows went up, and she stilled. "Do tell."

"I lied."

She looked surprised by that. "To me?"

"No. Not *to* you. But it was about you."

"What did you say? Something good, I hope. Did you tell some guy I was really smart and rich and hot?"

I knew I shouldn't smile, but I did. "No."

"Too bad. I could have faked that, at least for a little while."

"You are smart and hot."

She coughed out a laugh. "Maybe a little smart. And maybe a little hot. I'm sure not rich."

"Not yet."

"No, not yet. But back to your lie…"

"Right." I'd been framing up my words for the better

part of a day. I didn't know why I was trying to rephrase them on the fly right now. "I lied to Jamie about you calling me to say Brooklyn had a problem."

"Who's Jamie?"

"James. I mean James."

Sophie looked completely baffled. "What are you talking about?"

I took another drink. "I've been seeing James." Okay, that had come out all wrong. "I mean, not seeing him, as in seeing him. Just, well, with Brooklyn leaving him, and Henry leaving me, we kinda got to talking one day, and we've done a few things together."

"What kind of things?"

"Rock climbing, for one."

"You?"

"Yes."

"And James."

"Yes."

"*Rock* climbing?"

"We did. We took lessons and everything."

"Why didn't you tell me? How is that a secret? Was it illegal rocks? Were you trespassing? Did you steal something from…I don't know…Olympic National Park? A treasure or something?"

"We didn't steal anything."

"Well, that's a relief."

I knew I had to get to the point. "While we were in California, I—"

"You and James went to California?"

"Last weekend."

"Okaaay…" She drew out the word. "Did you, like, climb some California rocks?"

"No. He has that new job. We were house hunting."

Sophie sat back. She took a drink of her wine. "You do know you're not making any sense at all."

"I know."

"Tell me more about the lie."

"In California, in LA, I pretended you phoned me. I pretended Brooklyn had a problem. I knew he wouldn't ask any questions about Brooklyn, so I thought I'd get away with it."

"Did you get caught?"

"No. Not yet."

"I don't know, Nat. You're acting like this is a big thing. It doesn't sound like a big thing to me. I'll lie for you if you want me to. I'll tell him anything you say."

I knew she would, and I loved her for it.

"But why did you lie? What did it get you?"

"Out of there."

"Out of LA."

"Yes."

"You needed an excuse to leave?"

"I...thought I did in the moment."

Sophie sat forward and stared at me straight in the eyes. "What happened?"

I shook my head. "Some things I can't tell."

I wasn't sure if Jamie wanted to keep our makeover plot a secret. It didn't seem like such a big deal if we told people at this point. But I didn't want to break my word without getting his permission.

"What things can you tell me?"

"Jamie and I became friends."

"Jamie? He's Jamie now?"

"It's a nickname."

A knowing light came on in Sophie's eyes. "Like Tasha is for you. What *have* you two been up to?"

"Nothing... I mean..." I couldn't look at her.

There was awe in her tone. "Holy cow."

I could feel my face heat up.

"You slept with James Gillen? Nat, you slept with Brooklyn's fiancé?"

"They weren't engaged anymore. And it was nothing. It was a friends thing, friends with benefits thing."

"You have benefits with James?"

"Only a couple of times."

"Is that what happened in California?"

"No. It didn't happen in California. It would have. If I hadn't left."

"And you didn't want it to."

I wasn't sure how to answer that question, so I moved on. "And now he keeps texting and calling."

"Hang on," Sophie said, holding up a finger. "It sounds like you're saying you *wanted* to have benefits in California. So why did you leave?"

An ache formed in my stomach. "I didn't mean to tell you all this."

"Of course you meant to tell me all this. You must have been dying to tell me all this. Why did you wait so long to tell me all this?"

"It was a secret. It was a thing. It was a secret thing."

"James wanted to have a secret affair with you?"

"It wasn't an affair. Neither of us is with anyone."

"You were kind of dating Ethan."

I gave her a look. "Please."

"Okay. I guess you weren't really dating Ethan."

"It wasn't romantic," I said.

To my embarrassment, my voice cracked.

Sophie's eyes filled with sympathy.

"Oh," she said. "You mean it wasn't supposed to be romantic."

I struggled to breathe. I was afraid to try to talk. The

heartache I'd been suppressing was fighting to get out of my chest.

"But it got romantic."

A whisper was all I could manage. "Only for me."

I blinked against the threat of tears. I wasn't going to cry. I wasn't going to let this make me cry. That would be a whole other level of pain.

"Oh, Nat."

I shook my head, and I swallowed hard. "I'm fine. I just… I didn't want Jamie to ask you about the phone call and have him find out I made it all up."

"Yeah, because *that's* the biggest problem here."

"I'd be embarrassed," I said.

"He's the one who should be embarrassed. What was he thinking? Sleeping with you, swearing you to secrecy. What kind of a man does that?"

I realized I'd mischaracterized our relationship. I hadn't been fair to Jamie. This wasn't his fault. It was my fault for letting it get out of hand.

I should have pulled the plug earlier. I recognized the signs. I'd have to be an idiot not to recognize the signs that I was falling for him.

A knock came on the door.

I wasn't expecting anyone.

"Do Bryce and Ethan know you're here?" The last thing I wanted was to deal with anyone else right now.

"Maybe it's Brooklyn," Sophie joked.

I couldn't find the humor in it.

"Too soon?" she asked.

"I think it is."

"Tasha?" a voice called.

It was Jamie.

Sophie's mouth dropped open. Her voice dropped to a whisper. "I'm guessing nobody else calls you that?"

"Tasha, open up. I can hear you're in there."

I looked to Sophie for advice.

She cringed and shrugged at the same time.

"Tasha?" Jamie sounded frustrated. "This is ridiculous."

"She's coming," Sophie called out.

I shot her a look of astonishment.

"You can't hold him off forever."

I opened the door.

"*What* is going on?" Jamie asked.

"Sophie's—"

"You don't pick up the phone. You barely answer my texts. You said you were coming back. Why didn't you come back?" He barged into the apartment. "There were papers to sign."

He spotted Sophie.

"Hi, James," she said.

He clamped his jaw and glared at me.

"I can leave," Sophie said.

"No," I said.

I wasn't ready to be alone with Jamie. Okay, that was a lie. I was dying to be alone with Jamie. But that was a bad thing, a very bad thing.

Seeing him now, I wanted to grab him and hold on to him. I wanted to be wrapped in his arms…like…forever.

It was worse than I thought.

I was in love with Jamie.

"We need to talk," Jamie said to me.

I backed away from him. "She knows most of it anyway."

"What do you mean she knows most of it? What does she know?"

"*She's* right here," Sophie said. "Listening."

Jamie ignored her. "What does she know?"

"That we slept together."

"You told her that?"

"I pretty much guessed," Sophie said. "And why would you ask her to keep that a secret anyway?"

The question seemed to stump Jamie for a second. When he spoke, it was to me. "I didn't think you'd want to tell people. I don't care if anyone knows."

The conversation felt surreal. "Well…Sophie knows."

"Fine," he said. "Why didn't you come back? What did I do?"

I found the question more than absurd. "You moved to California."

He seemed puzzled. "Yeah…and I asked you to come with me. You said you would."

I almost laughed at that. "You asked me to help you *buy a house*."

"Uh-huh. A house. That we both loved. That we could live in. Together."

"Whoa," Sophie said. She came up on her knees and watched over the back of the sofa.

"You did not," I said to Jamie.

If he had…well…I would have… I didn't really know, but it would have been something different than what I had done.

Now my brain and my heart started fighting again, trying to work out what Jamie had meant, what Jamie meant now.

He took a few steps toward me. "Tasha, what did you think was happening between us?"

"Makeovers," I said. That much I knew for sure. "We wanted to attract the opposite sex."

"Really?" Sophie asked.

"We did attract the opposite sex," Jamie said. "We attracted each other."

I waved my hand. "You know what I mean. We were friends."

"With benefits," Sophie said.

We both looked at her.

"Should I go now?" she asked.

"Don't bother," Jamie said.

He took another step toward me. "I don't know how it went off the rails. I wish I'd said or done something different." He came closer. "I don't know how you feel about me, Tasha. But I have to think there's something there. I can't be in this all alone. It doesn't make sense. I'm wild about you, *wild* about *you*, intellectually, physically, romantically." He leaned in. "I want to be your best friend. I want to be your lover. And I want to do it all forever. Rock climb with me, dance with me, skydive with me, buy tuxes with me. It can be in LA. It can be here. It can be anywhere. I don't care about any of that." He took my hands. "I'm in love with you, Tasha."

"Swooning over here," Sophie said.

"Marry me," Jamie said.

My brain—which was already struggling to process his words—fogged completely over. "Huh?"

Jamie grinned at my baffled expression. "I think you have to give me a yes or no to that."

"Yes," Sophie said. "Say yes already."

Jamie cocked his head in Sophie's direction. "I like her. I always have."

"Yes," I said, barely believing it was happening. "I love you, Jamie. I love you so much."

He pulled me into a hug, and then a kiss, and then a deeper kiss.

"I'm out of here," Sophie said.

This time she didn't wait for either of us to answer.

* * *

Ours was going to be the simplest wedding in the history of weddings.

We both wanted it that way.

And we tried, we really did. But Sophie insisted Layla had to be there.

It was hard to argue that Jamie's sister shouldn't attend.

And if Layla was coming, Max had to be included. If Max and Layla were going to be there, it seemed churlish not to invite Brooklyn and Colton. Especially since Jamie was adamant that he didn't hold anything against Brooklyn.

He told me if it hadn't been for Brooklyn breaking up with him, he never would have found me. And he realized now that what he'd felt for Brooklyn had been puppy love. He'd hung on to it for so many years, he didn't know how to let it go, even when they grew apart.

He also said if it hadn't been for me, he wouldn't have grown from James into Jamie.

I believed him. I felt the same way. I wasn't Nat anymore. I wasn't only Tasha either, but I had a lot of Tasha in me, and I loved it.

Our parents had to be included, of course. Mine had traveled up from Houston.

Jamie's parents spent the winters in Fort Lauderdale now, but they were happy to put off their travel plans for a wedding.

Me, I just wanted to be married to Jamie. I didn't much care where or how.

We found a rustic resort on Waddington Island, an hour's boat ride from Seattle. It had a chapel overlooking the ocean, a five-star dining room, and cottages for everyone to spend the night.

I wore a short white dress, with a lace overlay and a scalloped hem. The lace neckline was scooped and detailed, while the underdress was strapless. I wore a little diamond pendant that Layla had lent me. Jamie had once given it to her for her birthday. I matched it with diamond stud earrings.

I felt pretty. I didn't think I'd ever felt this pretty in my life.

My shoes were sleek, heeled pumps, white with blue soles. Something blue. I liked that, too.

When the music came up, Sophie started down the aisle in front of me. She wore a simple aqua dress that let her beauty shine through. She looked amazing, as she always did.

I saw Jamie at the front of the chapel. He wore the tuxedo we'd bought together.

I smiled, and he grinned back, gesturing to the suit.

Yeah, I'd take a guy with a perfectly cut, perfectly fitting, owned tuxedo any day of the week—especially this guy.

"Nice touch," I whispered to him when I got to the front.

He took my hand. "Not as nice as you."

"Brookswood Bridal Department."

"Seriously?"

"Where else would I shop?"

"Friends…" the preacher began.

I sobered and stopped talking.

We said our vows, promising love and laughter and adventure forever.

When we kissed and made our way down the aisle, I thought my heart would burst open with joy.

In the garden out front, Layla hugged Jamie. Then she pulled me to her.

"I can't believe it," she whispered. "I'm *so* happy to have you as a sister."

"I love Jamie very much," I told her.

"I know you do. And I can see how much he loves you. You're perfect for each other."

Brooklyn was next.

I hesitated in front of her. We hadn't spoken since she'd left Jamie at the altar.

"Congratulations," she said. It was clear she was as nervous as me. I thought of all the platitudes I could offer.

"This is so weird," I said instead.

Her expression relaxed. "Isn't it?"

"I don't know how it happened this way. But I'm so glad it did." I pulled her into a hug.

"I do love James," she said into my ear. "Just not in the right way."

"I love him in exactly the right way."

She hugged me tighter. "I'm so happy for both of you."

"Thanks for leaving him," I said.

We both laughed.

"Do you think he wants to talk to me?"

Her question was answered before I could say anything. Jamie was there beside us.

"Hello, Brooklyn."

She looked up at him and stepped back from me. "Hi."

"Thanks for coming," he said.

"Thanks for inviting us."

They both fell silent.

"I'm sorry," she said.

Jamie shook his head. "I'm not. You were braver than me. I'd have gone ahead and made a mistake for both of us."

Brooklyn looked startled.

"You were right to walk away." He paused. "Okay,

maybe you could have done it a day or a week or a month before the wedding. But at least you did it." Jamie took my hand and drew me to his side. "And I'm the big winner."

"I'm so glad you feel that way," Brooklyn said.

I caught movement out of the corner of my eye as Colton approached.

I couldn't tell the twin brothers apart, but from the expression on his face, I was pretty sure this one was Colton, not Max.

He firmly stuck out his hand for Jamie. "Congratulations," he said.

"To you, too," Jamie said. "You have an amazing wife."

"I hear you lucked out, too." Colton looked to me.

Jamie wrapped an arm around me. "She's the best. I'm not sure I deserve her."

No one seemed to know where to take the conversation from there. I didn't want to leave it at this. Brooklyn was one of my best friends, and I was deliriously happy at how things had turned out.

"Thank you," I said to Colton. "I appreciate you stealing Brooklyn."

It was clear he had no idea how to react.

I let him hang for a second.

"I…uh…" He gamely stepped in. "It was my pleasure."

I looked around the circle. "We all agree it turned out right?"

Everyone enthusiastically nodded.

"Great. Then let's quit being so weird about it."

Jamie leaned in. "Way to go, Tasha."

"Tasha doesn't mess around."

"Yes," Brooklyn said with enthusiasm. "I'm through being weird."

"Okay by me," Jamie said.

He gave Brooklyn a hug.

They were both smiling when they pulled back.

Colton looked happy, too. He looked relieved and happy.

Other people came forward with their congratulations. We cut the cake, threw the bouquet and danced the night away under a full moon and the scattered stars.

Later, at our cottage on a point of land overlooking the rolling ocean, Jamie carried me across the threshold. An open window had the sea breeze flowing into the pretty room.

Jamie set me on my feet, his arm staying around my waist. He smoothed my windblown hair. "I love you, Tasha Gillen."

My heart was big and full in this perfect moment. I touched his face, stroking the rough whiskers that shadowed his chin. "I adore you, Jamie Gillen."

He smiled as he leaned in for a kiss. "I'd point at you across any old room."

* * * * *

If you missed Layla and Max's
unforgettable romance, and how Brooklyn
met Colton, check out Barbara Dunlop's
The Twin Switch,
available now from Harlequin Desire
at www.Harlequin.com!

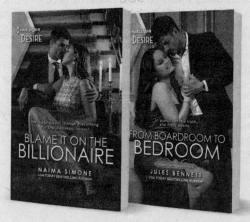

SPECIAL EXCERPT FROM

HQN

When India Robidoux needs help with her brother's high-profile
political campaign, she has no choice but to face the one man she's
been running away from for years—Travis, her sister's ex-husband.
One hot summer night when Travis was still free, they celebrated her
birthday with whiskey and an unforgettable kiss. The memory is as
strong as ever—and so are the feelings she's tried so hard to forget…

Read on for a sneak peek of
Forbidden Promises *by Synithia Williams*

"We need everyone else in the family to demonstrate that family and friendships are still strong despite the divorce. I'm pairing Travis up with Byron and India."

India's jaw dropped. Everyone turned to her. Everyone except Elaina, who stood even more rigid next to the window.

"Me? Why me?" The words came out in a weird croak and she cleared her throat.

"Because you make sense," Roy explained.

Travis crossed the room to the food. India quickly stepped out of his way. Her hip bumped the table, rattling the platters set on the surface. Travis raised an eyebrow. She forced herself to relax and nod congenially. She wasn't supposed to react when he was near. They were cool now. They'd cleared the air. Deemed what had happened years ago a mistake. She couldn't run and hide when he came near.

She focused on Roy. "What do I have to do?"

"There will be a few times when we'll need family members to campaign for Byron if he can't be there personally. We've got a lot of ground to cover, and if we can show a united front, I'd recommend having at least two family members together in those cases. I'll partner you with Travis for those appearances. The two of you can play up how great he is as a brother and friend."

Roy made it all sound so easy. Sure, everything seemed simple to everyone else. They didn't realize the easy friendship she'd once shared with Travis was gone. No one knew she could barely look at him without thinking about how she'd loved him. How she'd dreamed about his kiss even after he'd married Elaina. Fought to forget the feel of his hands on her body as she'd stood next to her sister at their wedding.

"Now that that's settled," Roy said, obviously taking India's silence as agreement, "we can get to the next point."

"Are you okay with spending time with me?" Travis asked in a low voice.

India's heart did a triple beat. He'd slid close to her as Roy moved on. His proximity was like an electric current vibrating against her skin.

"Of course," she said quickly. "Why wouldn't I be?"

"You wouldn't be the only person not wanting my company lately."

The disappointment in his voice made her look up. He wasn't looking at her. He frowned at the floor. His lips were pressed into a tight line. She wanted to reach out and touch him. To attempt to erase the sadness from his features. "I'll always want your company."

His head snapped up and he studied her face. She really shouldn't have said that. The words were too close to how she really felt.

"We'll need to pick out a suitable fiancée for him."

Roy's voice and the randomness of his words broke India from the captivating hold of Travis's eyes. She tuned back into the conversation. "Fiancée? Who needs a fiancée?"

Byron chuckled and placed a hand on his chest. "I do."

India looked from her father to Byron. Were they serious? "You didn't mention you were getting married."

Byron shrugged as if not mentioning a possible fiancée wasn't a huge deal. "I didn't decide to ask her until recently. We've been dating for a few months."

Dating for a few months? Wasn't he the same guy Travis had teased about three women calling him just yesterday? Her brother was a ladies' man, but he wasn't a dog. He wouldn't be considering marriage to someone if he still had multiple women calling his phone. Would he? Had he changed that much while she'd been gone?

She spun toward Travis. "You aren't letting him do this, are you?" She pointed over her shoulder at her brother.

Travis stilled with a chocolate croissant halfway to his mouth. "Do what?"

She stepped closer and lowered her voice. "Marry this Yolanda person. Who is she? Are they really dating?"

Travis sighed. "They've gone back and forth for a while."

Which really meant that her brother had been sleeping with her for a few months, but there was no commitment. Her hands balled into fists. She couldn't believe this!

"Don't spout off the campaign bullshit with me," she said in a low voice that wouldn't carry to her plotting relatives still in the room. "Not with me. This is a campaign maneuver."

"Roy has a point." Travis said the words slowly, as if he couldn't believe he was agreeing with Roy. "Your brother can't be a senator if he's out there picking up women in bars. He's got to settle down. Yolanda is who he chose."

"Did he choose her?" She wouldn't doubt that Roy, or their dad, picked the perfect woman for him.

"He said he chose her."

"Do you believe him?"

Travis glanced at the group huddled together. "I want to believe him. Giving up what you want for an unhappy marriage isn't worth the price of a senate seat." He turned a heavy gaze on her. "Not when it ruins a true chance at happiness."

India leaned back. She was stunned into silence. Her throat was dry and her stomach fell to her feet. The regret in his eyes created a deep ache in her chest. Had he given up something for an unhappy marriage? Before the words could spill from her lips, he took a bite of the croissant and strolled over to join the strategizing team, leaving India with another unanswered question to taunt her at night.

Don't miss what happens next in
Forbidden Promises by Synithia Williams!
Available February 2020 wherever
HQN books and ebooks are sold.

HQNBooks.com